MANHUNT

A BIGFOOT THRILLER

ERIC S BROWN

SEVEREDPRESS

MANHUNT

Copyright © Eric S Brown

WWW.SEVEREDPRESS.COM

ISBN: 978-1-922861-72-6

MANHUNT

The diner was finally quiet. The screaming had stopped as Dearil plunged the butter knife deep into the center of the blonde's throat. Dearil had her pinned to the floor beneath him. Her body bucked, spasming, blood bursting up and out of her lips, her remaining eye wide as she died. Dearil wiped at the warm red that had splattered on his face, smiling, as above him a fluorescent buzzed and flickered.

Life was funny, Dearil thought, a bloody rip roaring fun time too. . .If you were smart enough to grab hold of the chances it offered you. When the three marshals accompanying Dearil to his new "home"stopped at the diner he had never expected such a glorious opportunity to come his way. Within it, there was only the cook, two waitresses, and an old man sitting in a booth at the back of the establishment. The better looking of the two waitresses was a petite blonde and Dearil's eyes had instantly locked onto her. Fred, the marshal in charge, had noticed.

"Don't even think about it,"Fred warned.

As the other two marshals, Wallace and Benny, escorted Dearil to the restroom for a bathroom break, Fred met the approaching blonde to place their order. Dearil was hungry for a burger, dripping blood, but didn't get a vote in terms of what his late night meal would be.

Wallace opened the restroom door for him,"In you go."

Benny followed Dearil inside.

"Are you going to watch, Benny?" Dearil snickered. "Didn't get a good enough look last time, huh?"

"Shut up and do your business," Benny ordered him.

"It would help if you took off these cuffs," Dearil held up his bound hands towards the younger marshal.

"Not a chance in Hell, Dearil," Benny growled.

Dearil was blessed with a photographic memory, one of his many talents. He replayed the layout of the diner in his head while urinating in the stall with Benny standing only feet away from him. There was never going to be a better shot than now. Dearil zipped up his pants and made his move. Benny, though watching him, still never managed to see Dearil's move coming.

Stepping back away from the urinal, Dearil

staggered. In that instant, before Benny could process what was happening, he leapt at the marshal. His hands grabbed Benny's groin, fingers sinking into the soft flesh they found there as Dearil's head shot forward. Benny's scream was silenced as Dearil's teeth ripped out his windpipe. He backed up as Benny toppled over onto the nasty floor of the restroom. Dearil stomped on Benny's face, bringing his foot down with enough force for the sound of crunching bone to be heard.

The door to the restroom flew open, Wallace rushing inside, gun drawn. Dearil charged into him, knocking the marshal off balance. Wallace's finger squeezed the trigger of his pistol but the shot went wild. Dearil swept around him, slipping the chain of his cuffs over Wallace's head and bringing the metal taut against the flesh of his neck. Dearil held tight as Wallace struggled.

"Are you coming in next, Fred?" Dearil yelled as he cackled at Wallace's face turning blue.

Dearil was betting that Fred wouldn't. His entire plan hinged on it. It was a gamble but Dearil could read people like books and his bet was that Fred, with both of his men likely down, wouldn't risk coming himself. He'd remain outside, covering the door, and protecting the others in the diner.

Wallace went limp, the life choked out of him. Dearil's grin was feral as he heard Fred shouting outside the restroom. The marshal was playing perfectly into his hands. Frisking through Wallace's pockets Dearil found a key to his cuffs and set himself free.

"Dearil!" Fred yelled. "Get the hell out here now with your hands up!"

"Oh, I don't think so, Fred," Dearil shouted back and then muttered,"at least not yet" under his breath.

Fred's pistol cracked three times. Rounds struck the restroom door, punching holes through it. None of them even came close to where he was crouching above Wallace's body.

"Ah, ah, ah, Fred," Dearil laughed. "You'll have to do better than that."

Dearil moved quickly, taking up a position to the right of the door, getting into place as fast as he could in case Fred tried another volley. If Fred got brave and tried to come, he was a dead man. Dearil clutched Wallace's pistol in his right hand, rubbing at the wrist above where he held it with his left. The cuffs hadn't been kind to him.

"Really?" Dearil teased the marshal outside the restroom. "That's all you got?"

"Don't make this harder than it has to be, Dearil,"Fred barked. "Come out with your hands up. Now! The local flatfoots are on their way. There's no chance in Hell you're getting out of here."

"We'll see about that." Dearil looked at the bullet holes in the restroom door, thinking up his next move. The window was too small for him to fit through and there was no other way out. Somehow Fred knew that too. Likely the folks who worked in this grease trap had told him. Fred believed him cornered. The thing about cornered animals though is that they tend to fight harder than one would think.

Ducking down as he went, Dearil charged through the restroom door. As it swung open, Fred fired again. His first and only shot was high. Dearil heard it whistle over him then rose up, squeezing the weapon's trigger in rapid succession. Fred took a bullet to the chest and stumbled backwards. Dearil put two more into him before the marshal could recover. He knew Fred was wearing a vest beneath his shirt and jacket so the 9mm rounds weren't doing more than bruising him and knocking the air from his lungs. The fourth round took Fred to the floor. Fred fought to bring the barrel of his pistol up at Dearil but was too slow to get off a shot. Dearil kicked the weapon from the marshal's hand and then, placing a foot in the center of Fred's chest, stood above him.

"Bye, bye Fred," Dearil smiled, putting a final round into Fred's forehead.

"Please, mister!" one of the waitresses cried out.

"Don't hurt us!"

Dearil looked around. Both waitresses and the diner's cook were still in the building. The old man who had been at the table in the rear was outside in the parking lot, high tailing it for a rough looking pickup truck with flaking paint.

The cook tried to rush him. Dearil ended that with a single shot. The bullet entered the side of the cook's neck releasing an explosion of hot, wet blood in its wake.

The waitress who had cried out sunk to her knees on the diner's floor, weeping like a child, hands raised into the air. The other waitress though, the pretty petite blonde, bolted for the diner door. Dearil couldn't allow that. There was fun yet to be had. A shot to the back of her right leg stopped her very properly. She went down in a crumple of limbs.

"Stay where you are," Dearil ordered the two waitresses. "Move without me telling you to and well. . .you won't like what happens."

After that, Dearil had his fun with the two women . . . and now, that fun was at an end with both of them dead.

Dearil had popped one of the blonde's eyes out but the other was still intact. He couldn't resist such a tasty morsel before making his departure from the diner. Leaning over, Dearil punctured the surface of the eyeball with a fork and then placed his mouth over the eye as if kissing it, sucking out its juices.

Outside, the sound of screaming sirens could be heard, approaching from the south. Dearil paid them no heed. He conceived his plan of escape upon having the opportunity to do so arise. The diner was remote, very remote. It was on a road that cut through a large, untouched swathe of forests and hills. Dearil wasn't a true outdoors man but knew enough, he figured, to survive a trek through the woods, perhaps even a stay there, until he could emerge at a point of his choosing to re-enter the world again.

Under other circumstances, Dearil would have cleaned himself up from the blood slicked mess that he was but there was no need for that yet. Besides, the smell of his "fun" on him made Dearil happy. There would be no one in the woods to care. And if some animal came his way, he could deal with that.

Moving around the diner, Dearil found a backpack in the kitchen that must have belonged to the cook propped up near the back exit. He filled it hurriedly with anything that might be needed during his "time away" from both the diner and the bodies of the dead. As a trio of patrol cars with blazing lights pulled into the parking lot, Dearil crept out its backdoor. Darkness had fallen as if to indicate that even time itself was on his side. He sucked in a deep breath of night air and then merrily skipped his way towards the woods behind the diner without looking back. With any luck, he'd come across some campers and hikers in the days and nights ahead. Oh what fun to be had if he did. Licking his lips at such a wonderfully tasty thought, Dearil vanished into the depths of the trees.

****

The black Dodge Charger roared along the winding mountain. Stephen was at the wheel. Lucas sat in the passenger seat tapping his fingers nervously on the edge of his side's window. They both knew the kind of crapfest that lay ahead of them. This one wasn't your everyday, run of the mill gig even in their line of work. Three fellow marshals down, several other folks supposedly dead too, and a famous serial killer on the loose.

"Frag me, man," Stephen muttered as the diner came into view. The place was overrun by media vans, ambulances, and patrol cars. "This is gonna be bad."

"Just remember to smile for the cameras," Lucas quipped, putting on his game face as Stephen pulled the Dodge Charger into the lot outside of the diner.

No sooner had they stepped out of the car than they were swarmed by the press.

"Is it true that Dearil Horror is loose?" a reporter called out.

"Just how many people are dead in there?" another shouted, pointing at the diner.

"How does something like this happen?"

"How could Dearil escape like this?"

The questions just kept coming.

"No comment at this time!" Lucas barked back at the news people surrounding him.

He and Stephen made their way through the crowd and crossed the yellow tape the locals had put up around the diner. The reporters and spectators knew better than to follow them. A big, burly man with a graying black beard who was clearly the town sheriff was barking orders at his deputies.

"Sheriff Roland," Stephen said getting the big man's attention.

"Oh look who it is," Sheriff Roland growled. "Finally decided to show up, huh? Could have used you hours ago."

"We got here as fast as we could," Lucas cut in. "And we're the ones who lost three of our own in there, Sheriff. Best to keep that in mind."

Lucas's words hit the sheriff like a punch to his gut. The big man knew what it was like to lose friends in their line of work. The scowl on his face softened into a frown.

"Right," Sheriff Roland nodded as if in apology. "Best we get you two on inside. It's a bloodbath in there but you need to see it."

The sheriff led them into the diner through its front door. He wasn't kidding either. The entire floor of the diner appeared to be slicked with congealed blood. It was splattered everywhere too, the walls, the table, hell. . . there was even some spots of blood on the ceiling. Lucas counted four bodies, two female, two male. One of them he recognized as Fred Turner, the agent who had been in charge of Dearil Horror's transfer. Dearil had shot him in the head but Fred had still gotten off easy compared to the other three. Their bodies were mutilated and savaged in various ways. A man in a cook's apron lay on the floor, his gut slashed open, intestines yanked out of him by the handfuls and lay coiled about his corpse like bloated, red slicked, purple snakes. Both of the women were missing most of their clothes. The little blonde was also missing both of her eyes. Lucas, having read up on Dearil Horror, knew that he claimed to enjoy the taste of them and had undoubtedly sucked hers out. The other woman appeared to have been brutally raped, her short skirt pushed up above her thighs, her underwear was gone, and legs spread. Of course that wasn't all that had been done to her. Dearil had slit her throat from one side to the other and at some point slashed off her right breast as well. Lucas had to look away from her as bile rose up in his throat.

"God have mercy," Stephen muttered.

"Your other two guys are in the bathroom," Sheriff Roland told them. "Looks like Dearil took them out in there. They're intact. He didn't go back to mess them up like the poor folks out here. I'll give you a moment to look around. We can talk again after."

Sheriff Roland left the diner, his deputies clearing out with him.

"Fred had a wife and two kids," Lucas said, breaking the sudden silence that had fallen in the wake of the locals' departure. There was still plenty of noise outside but neither of them were paying any attention to it.

"Crappy way to go," Stephen agreed, staring at the gaping hole in Fred's forehead.

Stephen was single. If he got what Lucas was saying at all, Stephen didn't show it. Lucas wondered if he was so brash and uncaring before he got married too. He and Kristen had been together for almost two years. There was no doubt she had changed him, from his core outward. Lucas knew thinking about her was the last thing he needed to be doing right now. It would just screw up his head and keep him from focusing like he should. Dearil Horror was the most dangerous man the two of them had ever been sent to bring in. . . and it wasn't going to be easy.

Lucas and Stephen took a look around. Stephen headed into the restroom where Dearil had taken out the other two agents while Lucas examined the bodies in the main diner. The level of sadistic joy Dearil inflicted upon the two women was utterly inhuman. Lucas didn't believe that anyone was purely evil but if there were a human that was, Dearil Horror was likely in the running for that title.

Stephen emerged from the restroom a few minutes later as Lucas was kneeling next to the body of the little blonde waitress corpse. "You good?"

He could hear the concern in his partner's voice.

"Yeah," Lucas answered, rising to his feet. "I'm as good as I am going to be until we find the sicko that did this and bring him in."

"Nobody said that we had to bring him in alive," Stephen pointed out since it was just the two of them in the diner.

"Guess we'll see how it goes." Lucas looked over to see the rage burning in Stephen's eyes. There were agents who didn't mind taking out scum like Dearil Horror if they got the chance but Lucas wasn't one of them. As terrible and inhuman as what the man had done was, Lucas still believed in the law. If he didn't, Lucas would never have become a U.S. Marshal.

"The locals say he was gone from the scene when they arrived," Stephen said. "It did take them a while to get here. This place is pretty remote."

"Yeah but you can see how Dearil spent most of that time by just looking around," Lucas frowned.

"There was one survivor," Stephen told him. "An old man named Ditko. Supposedly he ran like Hell and got out of here in his truck before Dearil went to town on these folks. According to his statement, the last time Ditko saw Dearil, he was still in this diner."

"That doesn't tell us anything," Lucas said.

Stephen pulled a pack of cigarettes from his pocket and lit one up. He still smoked, unlike Lucas. Usually, Stephen kept it to a minimum around him but right now, Lucas could see that Stephen really needed a smoke. Hell, he did too but wasn't picking up that habit again. It was too hard to break the first time. Lucas knew he might never stop if he started again.

"I know that look," Stephen commented, exhaling a mouthful of smoke. "What are you thinking?"

Lucas cocked his head slightly, looking out at the

parking lot. The local authorities assumed Dearil had stolen a car from the lot and was headed out of state. Procedure dictated that they set up road blocks and lock down the nearby airports. Lucus figured something else entirely.

"I don't think Dearil took a car from that lot," he frowned. "As smart as he is, Dearil would know the standard playbook for a fugitive hunt like this like the back of his hand."

"So what the hell do you think he did then?" Stephen grunted. "Just teleported away?"

"No," Lucas answered. "I think he just pulled a Bundy."

"Frag me," Stephen moved closer to the diner's front window, staring out of it.

Lucas walked over to stand next to him. "I'd wager Dearil had his fun in here, loaded up with anything and everything he could, and then bolted straight up into those mountains."

"And I assume we're going in after him then?" Stephen asked.

"Yep," Lucas nodded, "but first we're going to get some proper gear and some help."

****

Dearil spent most of the night moving as fast as he could, putting as much distance between himself and the diner as possible. His plan was simple: hide out in the woods for a bit and then he would slip back into the world outside of them at a point of his choosing. He was exhausted. His legs ached with each step further that he took. Not willing to risk injury by pressing on with the world around still mostly dark. Moving at night was rough enough. Stumbling around in the darkness too tired to think properly was like asking for a costly mistake to happen. Glancing at a watch taken from the body of the lead agent of those who had been transporting him, Dearil saw that it was pushing 4 AM.

A feral cry rang out from somewhere to the south between where he was and the diner. Dearil had heard it before during the night but at first thought it was just his tired mind playing tricks on him. The sound was too human in nature to be any sort of animal but at the same time, no human could have ever produced such a noise. It was sort of a deep, guttural cry more akin to that of an ape than any woodland creature Dearil could think of. It sure as hell wasn't a coyote or a wolf. Dearil had never heard a bear in real life before but even so, his instincts told the killer that wasn't what was making the noise either though that would have fit the deepness of the sound. The cry was distant and that was the important thing about it at the moment.

Whatever was out there, it wasn't close enough at hand to worry about . . . yet.

Dearil kept staggering forward, sweat dripping from his hair into his eyes, before coming across a small clearing in the woods. It seemed as safe a place to stop for a bit as any. Shrugging off his pack, Dearil set it down on the ground next to the trunk of a wide tree. He rubbed at his eyes with the backs of his hands and then shook his head to clear it. The cries had fallen silent. Dearil was smart enough to know that didn't mean anything. There was no telling what the thing that was making them was up to or which way it was headed. Dearil could only hope that the creature was nocturnal and would be getting some rest too as the sun came up. The first weak rays of the dawn were beginning to spill in through the shadows among the trees. He took a seat, leaning against the trunk of the tree he'd set his pack beside. It was good to be off his feet. Reaching over, Dearil dug a bottle of water out of his pack and twisted off its top. He chugged half the bottle in a single go. Staying hydrated was important. It helped one think more easily and clearly. Dearil breathed more easily, closing his eyes, still clutching the now half empty water bottle in his left hand. It was difficult to open his eyes after shutting them, as tired as he was, but Dearil did it. Piddling with the watch on his wrist, he set an alarm for 7 AM. That was plenty of time to get some rest in and still get back on the move before anyone could catch up to him. Dearil was betting it would take anyone coming after him a while to figure out that he hadn't stolen a car and launched out of the diner that way. Even if whoever they sent to lead the chase after him was smart enough to discern that he had done no such thing, it was unlikely that such an agent or officer would charge into these woods without taking the time to do it properly. . . and that would take time. Finishing his water, Dearil let the bottle fall to the ground and slumped against the tree, closing his eyes again. Sleep came quickly and was filled with the sweet, sweet memories of the two waitresses in the diner whimpering and shrieking.

The alarm Dearil had set woke him up. He jerked awake, ready for a fight. There was nothing to fight though. He was alone in the clearing just as he had been as he fell asleep. Neither his pursuers or whatever animal that seemed to have been stalking him in the night had caught up to him. Dearil sucked in a deep breath of morning air. His lips spread in a smile. It was good to be alive and free. Getting to his feet, Dearil stretched and popped his back. Sleeping against the tree hadn't been kind to it. The rest had done him wonders though. Dearil felt refreshed and ready to take on the world.

Moving quickly, Dearil hefted his pack onto his shoulders and got started back on his trek northward. The air was crisp and cool. His breath was visible in it but Dearil wasn't freezing. He learned the trick to dealing with cold a long time ago. If you simply accepted it and didn't fight it in your mind, it was an easy feeling to suppress. His pace wasn't the headlong dash of the night before but Dearil kept up a decent amount of speed with his walk. Gnawing on a power bar taken from the diner's kitchen as he went, Dearil took in his surroundings now that he could see them in the light of day. The terrain was anything but friendly. Roots that protruded up through the soft forest soil, thick grass, and dips in the ground itself made him wonder how he hadn't broken a leg or worse during his flight the night before. Dearil would have said that God was with him but that would have been a lie. The two of them were far from being on good terms. If there was any sort of divine power aiding him, some entity such as Shiva or Kali would have been its source, not God of the Christians. No, Dearil thought, correcting himself, he had merely rolled the bones and gotten lucky.

Dearil knew the day would warm up quickly and soon enough the heat would be bearing harshly down on him as the sun continued to rise in the sky.

He pressed on for several hours until sweat soaked his clothes and his muscles burned. The sun had reached its zenith in the sky when the smell hit his nostrils. It was a smell Dearil knew well. Another person would've been utterly sickened by it but not him. The stench of rotting flesh was being carried on the breeze from somewhere up ahead. Dearil stopped. There was no rush and proceeding with caution was the wisest way to play things. Dearil pulled out the pistol stuffed in his jacket pocket, readying the weapon. It was just a standard issue, 9mm Glock. If he ran into a large predator like a bear, the pistol wouldn't be much help. Still, it was all he had short of going hand to hand with a knife against any creature that might be waiting for him.

Creeping forward as stealthily as he could, Dearil approached the area where the smell was coming from. The woods opened up into a clearing larger than the one he had slept in. It contained someone's campsite. In the clearing's center sat a tattered tent. There was the remains of a fire that still smoldered. Strewn about in front of the tent was what was left of two human bodies. Not seeing any sign of whoever or whatever had killed them, Dearil crept on into the campsite. As he drew closer, Dearil saw that one of the bodies was a man and the other a woman. The man's head was missing. A piece of white spinal column jutted out from the bloody stump that was the man's neck. The woman lay on her back, spread out on the ground, the entire front of her body torn apart. Her ribs were cracked open and chords of intestines, red slicked, purple snakes, baked in the heat of the sun. It was easy to see that something had eaten portions of her entrails. One of the woman's arms was missing entirely. It hadn't been cut off of her but rather yanked away with brutal, savage strength. Dearil stood staring at the carnage in front of him. The woods surrounding him suddenly felt truly unsafe for the first time since he had entered them. A hunting rifle rested next to the headless corpse of the man. Dearil wondered if he'd gotten to use the weapon before having his head torn off. There was only one way to know for sure.

Dearil squatted and picked up the dead man's rifle. It was a bolt action, .30-.06. He was familiar with the weapon. It was a round short and there was evidence that the dead man had managed to shoot at whatever attacked him. Whether he had hit or missed was impossible to discern though. A .30-.06 packed a hell of a lot more of a punch than Dearil's Glock though so if the man had hit the thing that killed him perhaps he'd at least wounded the beast. Dearil was sure now that whatever had left the campers as mangled as they were wasn't another human. As to what sort of beast the thing might be though, he didn't have a clue. Whatever it was had to have an insane level of strength but also an uncanny amount of speed. Swinging the .30-.06 onto his own shoulder by its strap, Dearil kept his pistol in hand, rising up to his feet. As he did, Dearil noticed the tracks. All around the campsite were deep impressions in the soft ground. He was no tracker but they were too large and obvious to overlook. Sucking in a stunned breath, Dearil's mind reeled at what he was seeing.

"No," Dearil muttered, shaking his head. Everything inside of him told Dearil that he had lost his mind because what he was seeing couldn't possibly be real. He slapped his own face hard, blinking as his hand made impact. When he reopened his eyes, the tracks were still there. Dropping onto his knees, Dearil switched his pistol over to his left hand and placed his right inside the closest track. The track was massive. It was far larger than his hand. Based on its depth, whatever left it had to weigh over five hundred pounds, maybe even over half a ton. Dearil shuddered, a sudden chill rushing through him despite the heat of the day. There was only one creature Dearil knew of that could leave tracks like these. . . and it wasn't real.

****

Lucas and Stephen stood looking over the motley crew of individuals assembled in front of them. There were six of them in total. Eliza, in Lucas's opinion, was a very attractive dog handler. With her were her dogs Zek, Issac, and Stanton. Her dogs were supposed to be the best in the area and Sheriff Roland had hooked them up with her. Next was Trevor, a local tracker who often worked with Roland's department. Trevor was a twitchy little fellow but had proved his worth time and time again to Roland over the years. If anyone could track Dearil Horror through the mountains, the sheriff swore it was Trevor. Roland has also given them three of his deputies as muscle and extra bodies. Their names were Hedrick, Arey, and Wolfman. Hedrick stood out as the obvious leader among them. Though only in his twenties, he was confident, mentally quick, and appeared in overall great shape. Arey was a lithe woman. She couldn't weigh more than one-hundred-and-ten pounds, maybe even less than that. Lucas could see the toughness in her eyes though and hear it in her voice when she spoke. The woman was likely a lot more lethal than Hedrick ever would be. She was in her twenties too with short cropped black hair and piercing green eyes. Wolfman rounded out the trio of deputies. He was a hulking figure. Standing over six feet tall, the big man looked to be all muscle, like a weightlifter on steroids. His shoulders were wide and the thickness of his arms seemed to threaten to tear through the cloth of his uniform. And lastly there was Debra, a local EMT that they were bringing along in order to be safe if anything happened in the woods that required immediate medical attention. Debra was older, likely in her early forties, but she was experienced and knowledgeable with dozens upon dozens of rescue operations under her belt. Lucas was sure she'd be one hell of an asset to the group. All of them were just as restless and ready to go as Eliza's dogs, who were straining at her hold on them.

Sheriff Roland had fully taken over the crime scene again which left Lucas and Stephen in charge of the search at this point as it should be. Lucas wished they had a few more bodies but wasn't about to wait any longer. Dearil had enough of a jump on them as it was. Odds were the serial killer had been moving as fast as he could throughout the night. On foot, in the dark, and in unfamiliar woods, Lucas hoped that jump wasn't too large though. Still, Dearil hadn't managed to kill all the people he had in his career by being stupid or lazy. Dearil Horror's file attributed over three hundred deaths to the sicko and earned him a death sentence. He was being transferred to a facility where that sentence could be carried out when everything had gone to Hell and the poor souls inside the diner had paid the price for Fred and his team letting Dearil get the better of them.

"At this point, we're assuming Dearil headed north when he made a break for it," Lucas told the assembled group. "We'll start out in that direction and see if Eliza's dogs can pick up his scent. We can't stress enough how slippery and dangerous this perp is so we're all going to need to be careful out there and stay together as much as we can. Does everyone understand the plan?"

"Why north?" Deputy Wolfman asked.

"That's the direction that makes the most sense," Trevor answered in a nasally voice before either Lucas or Stephen could. "The route might be harder in some areas but it's the only direction that would truly take our guy deeper into the woods and we can bet that's where he wants to go for now. Away from the world, out among the trees, so that we can't find him. It's what I would do if I were him."

"Right," Stephen nodded. "So gather up whatever gear you need. We're moving in ten."

With that said, the group broke up to make their final preparations. Lucas sighed.

"What?" Stephen shot him a look. "You're not happy with the plan?"

"No. No, that's not it," Lucas answered. "Hell,

it's my plan, most of it anyway. I just have a bad feeling about this one, Stephen. I don't think we're going to be coming back from it."

"You need to get it together, man," Stephen shook his head. "This Horror guy is a sicko, sure, but it's just another gig and no matter how much the press likes to hype him up, he's still just another killer."

Lucas shrugged. "We should let the sheriff know we're rolling."

"Yeah," Stephen nodded. "I'll handle it."

Watching Stephen walk away to deal with Sheriff Roland, Lucas stood there frowning. His gut told him this was all going to go terribly. He couldn't put his finger on why exactly but Lucas had learned to trust his instincts over the years. Heading for their car, Lucas opened its trunk. Reaching in, he picked up both of the 12.5 inch barrel, Remington 870s. Lucas figured they would be needing the shotguns before all was said and done.

The dog handler, Eliza, and the tracker, Trevor, were standing behind him when Lucas shut the trunk and turned around.

"This guy we're after. . ." she said, "is he really as bad as you let on?"

"And then some," Lucas confirmed.

"It's not so much your guy I'm worried about if we're being honest," Trevor huffed.

Lucas gave the tracker a questioning glance. "What?"

"Don't you start again," Eliza warned Trevor. Lucas could tell the two of them had worked together before. That made sense given their connection to Sheriff Roland's department.

"You know it's out there, Eliza," Trevor scowled at her. "You just don't want to admit it."

"Whoa," Lucas stopped their bickering. "Anyone want to clue me in as to what you're arguing about?"

"You don't know anything about those woods, do you, Marshal?" Trevor asked him point blank.

Lucas shook his head. "Not really."

"Dozens of folks, hikers, campers, even hunters, go missing in them every year, mostly in this season too," Trevor told him.

"That doesn't mean. . ." Eliza started but Trevor held up a hand at her.

"He asked me, Eliza, not you," Trevor said. "Look, Marshal, according to local legends there's a monster out there somewhere in that woodland. A big, freaking, angry monster that kills anyone it comes across."

Lucas just stared at the little tracker blankly, waiting for more of an explanation because what Trevor just said was insane. There were no such things as monsters in the real world. . . except the human ones.

"Trevor believes that there's a feral Sasquatch out there," Eliza blurted out as if unable to stop herself.

"Yeah, I do!" Trevor snapped at her. "Sure, I've never seen the thing or met up with it personally but. . ."

"But you've seen the tracks," Eliza rolled her eyes.

"I have!" Trevor stood his ground, unrelenting.

Lucas put a hand on Trevor's shoulder. "Trevor, isn't it?"

The tracker nodded. "Yes sir."

"You have to know what you're saying sounds utterly whacko, right?" Lucas told him.

"There's evidence. . ." Trevor started.

"It's clear you really believe in what you're saying, Trevor, but right now, there's a very real monster in those woods and it's up to us to bring that bastard in before he hurts anyone else. I appreciate your warning but we have to keep our heads level and focused on the job ahead of us so let's not bring this up with the others."

Eliza snorted. "Trust me, Marshal, the deputies know all about Trevor's theories. Everyone around here does. They won't be bothered by them."

"Hey now!" Trevor almost went at her.

"Trevor. . ." Lucas said sternly. "Regardless, like I said, we need to keep our focus on Dearil

Horror, above all else. Can you do that?"

"Of course. I'm a professional and I know what we're heading out there for, Marshal. I'll find your man. Count on it," Trevor seemed insulted but Lucas believed him.

****

The group left just after dawn. Eliza let her dogs lead her into the woods as everyone else followed along behind her. Trevor was on her heels, eyes alert, scanning everything around them. The three deputies brought up the rear with Debra, the EMT. Lucas and Stephen carried their Remington 870s in addition to their normal sidearms. Hedrick was packing an AR-15 while Arey was armed with a high powered, bolt action sniper rifle. The big deputy, Wolfman, gripped a pump action 12 gauge in his huge, calloused hands. They all kept a brisk but cautious pace.

Stephen watched Eliza and Trevor ahead of them.

The day was hot and humid. Lucas was thankful despite the heat. Rain would have been the worst thing that could have happened in terms of weather so Lucas was content to suffer in the rays of the sun just so long as the sun stayed out and dark clouds didn't roll in. Lucas had to admit, though he was a city boy and not overall a fan of the outdoors, that the area they were in was beautiful.

They had been hoofing it into the woods for a couple of hours before Stephen finally couldn't take the silence anymore.

"That little guy. . ." Stephen cocked his head over at Lucas, his voice low, "I heard he's got some issues. Just what kind of nutjob did the sheriff stick us with?"

"He'll get the job done," Lucas assured his partner. "Don't worry about it."

Stephen looked doubtful but trusted Lucas's judgment to let it go and change the subject. "That dog lady is hot," he said with a smirk on his face.

Lucas frowned.

"Hey," Stephen chuckled. "You're married not dead, man. You can still take in the sights."

Ignoring what Stephen said, Lucas glanced at his watch. "I'd say Dearil has at least a seven hour jump on us. We really need to be moving faster."

"Tell that to them," Stephen snorted, gesturing at Eliza and Trevor.

Lucas walked a bit faster, leaving Stephen behind, to catch up to Eliza.

"How's it going?" Lucas asked her.

"You asking about my dogs or me?" she grinned.

"I mean have they picked up Dearil's scent yet?" Lucas kept his eyes locked on hers, keeping tight control over where they wandered. Eliza was attractive but he refused to be an immature pig about it like Stephen.

"Hard to tell yet," Eliza answered honestly. "It's their show, ya know?"

The dogs suddenly came upon something that set them off. They started barking and straining at their leashes.

"They've got something now!" she laughed. "Go get 'em, boys!"

Eliza let her dogs loose. They darted on farther into the woods ahead of the group. Everyone charged after them. There was no keeping up with the dogs though, not in these woods. The ground was too rough terrain where they were.

Lucas heard the dogs come to a stop not too far in the distance. As the group caught up to them, Stephen and Hedrick took the lead with Wolfman right behind them. They were the first three to see what the dogs had found.

"Fragging Hell!" Hedrick shouted.

The dogs had surrounded a massive black bear. The animal was dead and sprawled out on the ground. Something had beaten the hell out of it and torn the bear open. Its entrails were spilled onto the grass around its corpse. The bear's head was bent at an unnatural angle, the white, jagged end of a bone sticking out through the hair and flesh of its neck.

Wolfman, the big deputy, had gone pale.

Eliza set about hurriedly rounding up her dogs and getting them under control. Trevor rushed straight to the bear and dropped down to look it over. Hedrick thumped Wolfman in the back and the two of them took up positions watching the trees so that Trevor could do his thing.

Lucas noticed Debra shudder as if a chill ran through her.

"You okay?" Lucas asked the medic.

"No," Debra answered, not holding back her feelings. "What the hell could kill a bear like that?"

"A Sasquatch did this," Trevor piped up from where he knelt next to the dead bear. "Had to be. Look at how this thing's neck is broken."

Lucas knew Eliza would have exploded on the little tracker but she was too busy with her dogs. She was having a difficult time with them as if something was spooking them. Stephen went after Trevor in her place though.

"Ah cut the crap, man!" Stephen barked at Trevor. "We didn't haul your arse out here so you could rant on about monsters that don't exist."

"Maybe he's right," Deputy Arey cut in unexpectedly.

Stephen's head whipped around in her direction.

"What?"

"We get so many reports of people missing out here," Deputy Arey said. "We've found more than our share of mutilated bodies too. Always put them down as animal attacks, you know, a bear, a big cat, whatever... but maybe there is something more going on."

"Deputy Arey," Hedrick snapped, silencing her.

Lucas eyed Hedrick. His gut feeling was that the lead deputy knew more than he was letting on.

"Deputy Hedrick," Lucas walked closer to him. "Is there something you might want to share with us?"

"No sir," Hedrick kept his voice level in his response despite his sudden anger with Deputy Arey.

Stephen picked up on how the lead deputy was holding something back too and leaped into the verbal sparring match. He aimed the barrel of his Remington 870 at Hedrick.

"I suggest you start talking right now, Deputy," Stephen growled. "We ain't screwing around out here and I, for one, don't plan on getting killed because you were keeping quiet about something."

"What the hell?" Hedrick balked at the sight of a US marshal aiming a shotgun at him. "You're not gonna shoot me."

"I wouldn't push him if I were you, Deputy,"

Lucas said playing the "good" cop. "His last agency required psych profile almost got his badge taken from him."

"Just tell them," Wolfman grunted. "Ain't gonna hurt nothin'."

"Fine," Hedrick relented. "Look, Arey's right. There's a lot of strange crap that happens out here. Those crypto folk come to the area all the fragging time looking for Bigfoot or whatever. A decent bit of them. . .well, they never make it home and we're left playing clean up. Still, that doesn't prove anything. There are bears, big cats, and even wolves in these woods."

"You've seen some of those bodies yourself, Hedrick," Arey glared at him. "You know more than a few of them weren't killed by any of those animals. Whatever got them was stronger and smarter."

"Frag me," Stephen shook his head. "You've got to be yanking my chain. There ain't no such thing as a Sasquatch already!"

"Hold up," Lucas stopped his partner. "I agree with you that Bigfoot doesn't exist but that doesn't change the fact there does appear to be evidence of something in these woods that's killing people. Let's just accept that and not put a name on whatever it is for now."

"If it walks like a duck and quacks like a duck,"

Trevor grinned from ear to ear.

"Give it a rest, Trevor," Deputy Arey frowned. "They aren't ready to hear what you're saying yet."

"Seems like I won you over though," Trevor chuckled. "I'll call that a win for today."

"How long has that bear been dead?" Lucas asked, changing the subject.

"I reckon a day or so at most," Trevor answered.

"So whatever killed it. . ." Lucas started.

"Is likely still in the area," Trevor confirmed. "Large predators tend to stick to the same killing grounds."

Debra had moved closer to the dead bear. "Would you look at those wounds. Whatever it was really tore into it after breaking its neck."

"Tore into it?" Stephen asked.

"Are you blind or something? She means the Sasquatch ate part of the bear, Marshal," Trevor explained.

Lucas stepped quickly to shove the barrel of Stephen's shotgun towards the ground.

"Let it go," he whispered and then raising his voice, addressed the group. "We've seen enough here. Eliza, are your dogs ready to get back to it?"

"As they're gonna be, Marshal," Eliza said. "I think I'm gonna need to keep 'em leashed this time though."

"Understood," Lucas motioned for everyone to

get moving behind Eliza and her dogs as they continued northward, deeper into the woods.

****

Steal My Sunshine by Len blared in Jason's earbuds. His head bobbed in time with the song's beat as he tugged on his boots. It hadn't been his idea to come out here. That was all Anne. She was likely furious that he had slept in so long today. Finishing up with his boots, Jason turned to look at the flap of the tent. Jason nearly jumped out of his skin as he saw Anne at the entrance, glaring at him. Her lips moved but he couldn't hear what she was saying over his music. Jason yanked his earbuds out.

"What?" he asked.

"I said get your sorry arse out here!" Anne fumed and then vanished from his line of sight.

Jason scrambled out of the tent. Will and Heather were all sitting around where last night's fire had been, eating a late lunch. From the frowns on their faces, they were likely ticked at him too. Jason knew he'd really gotten hammered last night but then wasn't that the point of coming out here? To get away and unwind?

"Wow, mate," Will eyed him. "Finally woke up, did you?"

It took effort not to make a smart comment but Jason bit his tongue and kept calm for Anne's sake. "Sorry, man," was all he said.

"Now that Jason's up, can we finally start breaking down the camp?" Heather asked.

"What?" Jason blinked. "I thought we were staying another day at least."

"No, Jason," Anne told him. "Today's the day we planned to head back."

"Oh," Jason looked around at the trees, intentionally not making eye contact with the others, especially Anne, "I guess I lost track of the days."

"Yeah well, don't sweat it too much, mate," Will got up, setting down a plate with a half eaten hot dog on it. "Let's just get started, eh?"

"Sure," Jason nodded. He felt like crap and still wasn't fully awake. "But could I get some coffee first?"

"There isn't any," Anne said sternly. "We drank that at breakfast, Jason."

"Right," Jason glanced up at the sky. The sun hurt his eyes but he could see that it was likely around noon.

The four of them went to work taking down the two tents and gathering up their gear. There was no banter or friendly playing like there had been when they were set up. Jason realized he must have ruined the end of their camping trip for all of them. Wondering just what in the devil he'd done last night to tick everyone off at him so much, Jason worked without complaining. Their camp was small and gear limited now that they'd used up pretty much all the supplies brought along for the trip so it didn't take much time to get the job done.

"Reckon we've got a few hours of daylight left," Will commented.

"Not enough to make it all the way back to the truck before nightfall," Heather sighed.

The blonde was a city girl through and through. She was a sharp contrast to Anne. Her body was soft and far more curvy. Not that Anne wasn't in her own way. Anne was just more fit and certainly was far more comfortable with the outdoors. Jason knew Heather hadn't really wanted to come on this outing any more than he had himself. The whole thing was Anne and Will's idea. Jason couldn't help but wonder why in the Hell the two of them weren't together instead of wasting their time with him and Heather. For Will, maybe it was that Heather was the sort of girl that some guys dreamed about. Not too sharp on the uptake and built like a brick house. She was hot. Even he had to admit that. Of course, Heather could be very petulant and immature but one could argue she was worth putting up with those things.

"Come on," Anne said, already headed into the

trees.

"Sucks to be you, I reckon," Will told Jason quietly as he passed by.

Heather didn't speak to him at all. Hell, she didn't even look at him.

Jason fell in behind the others. He needed to talk to Anne, see if things could be smoothed over between them somehow or at least find out what he had done that earned him such anger and disdain. He had never been a mean drunk so Jason figured something bad must have slipped out of his often, though not today, overactive mouth.

They all walked in silence. Jason's music was turned off and silenced, his earbuds dangling around his neck. Heather was listening to something though. Will was taking in the scenery while Anne just kept on marching through the trees without bothering to even glance back at them.

"Oh my gosh!" Heather suddenly stopped, shouting, jerking her earbuds out. "You're not going to believe what I just heard!"

Everyone stopped with her.

"There's a freaking serial killer loose in these woods," Heather blurted out.

Anne rolled her eyes. "Heather, we don't have time for this crap if we're going to get anywhere near reaching the truck today."

"I'm not screwing with you guys," Heather said.

"I was trying to find the weather and this news report cut in. Some freak named Dearil Horror escaped custody and is supposed to be loose in these mountains."

Will whistled, "Dearil Horror. That guy is hardcore."

"So you believe her now?" Anne snapped.

"Ain't no way she pulled that name out of the air," Will nodded. "She had to have heard it like she said."

"I'm right here," Heather snarled, insulted, "I can hear you, ya know?"

"Whatever," Anne blew her off.

"Honey, what did the news say?" Will asked, walking to put an arm around Heather, pulling her close to him. "Exactly."

Heather shoved him off. "Oh, so now you care."

"Heather. . ." Will pleaded. "I didn't mean. . ."

"I know you all think I'm an idiot," Heather was on the verge of tears but there was nothing but anger in her voice. "Well, screw you all."

"I don't think you're an idiot, Heather," Jason said.

Heather's head snapped around towards him, surprised. Then she settled down a bit.

"Thank you, Jason," Heather said.

"Yay! Now that you two have had your moment,

Jason, can we get the hell out of here?" Anne snarled.

Jason flinched. Leave it to Anne to get jealous even when she was ticked at him. With a heavy sigh, he answered, "Sure. Let's go."

Will walked by him, roughly bumping a shoulder into him. Jason grunted from the impact but otherwise didn't respond to what Will had done. Everyone was angry enough already without the two of them ending up in a brawl. Jason wasn't a fighter anyway. Odds were Will would tear him a new one if the two of them came to blows.

Falling in behind Will, Jason marched into the woods with Anne beside him. Heather brought up the rear of the group. There was no proper trail. Thankfully, between Anne and Will, they didn't need one to find their way back. Both of them were experienced outdoors people.

An inhuman roar rang out, echoing amid the trees from somewhere to the east. Everyone stopped.

"What the hell was that?" Anne asked, looking to Will.

He shrugged. "Never heard anything like it."

"Anne?" Jason turned to her, nerves on edge from the creepy noise.

"It wasn't a bear," Anne said, still focused on Will.

"I know that," Will snapped back at her. "But that doesn't mean I know what it was!"

Heather ran up to Will, throwing herself against him. He didn't resist her, taking Heather into his arms.

"Will, are we in trouble? Is it coming for us?" Heather begged for him to tell her that they were safe.

"We should be fine, honey," Will assured her. "Whatever it is, it's a long way off."

Jason could see from Anne's expression that she didn't agree with Will at all. She didn't argue with him though.

"Let's keep moving," Anne said and took the lead, walking by Will who still had his arms around Heather.

Anne's face was grim. It worried Jason a lot. If she was spooked and keeping it to herself, just what the hell was out there?

The group kept pushing through the woods, heading in the direction of where they had left the truck on one of the dirt roads to the south. They hadn't heard anything more. The one cry had been it. That creeped Jason out too as they walked. The lack of hearing another cry might mean whatever made it was gone, left behind as they kept going, or it could mean the animal had simply gone silent for some reason.

No one was ready, not even Anne, when the beast came bursting out of the woods towards them. All of them were utterly stunned. The thing was at least eight foot tall, moving on two legs. It was covered in filthy hair with massive, thick muscles beneath. Yellows eyes burned with rage as the giant, human-like beast charged at Heather. Will had a machete sheathed on the side of his backpack. He yanked it free, rushing to intercept the monster. Anne was carrying a hatchet and jerked it loose from her belt. Not a single one of them had a gun. None of them had thought they would need such a weapon in these woods. Heather was screaming, scared out of her mind. Jason didn't have a freaking clue what to do so he stood frozen, watching things play out.

Will met the monstrous beast head on, swinging his machete with all the strength he could muster. Its blade bit into the thing's shoulder. If the creature even noticed, it showed no sign of it. With a backhand swipe of its left hand, Will's head was torn from atop his neck by the force of the blow. Blood exploded upwards from the stump where his head had sat as it was sent flying away into the woods. Seeing Will die in such a fast and brutal manner snapped Jason out of his state of shock and into motion. He loved Anne. He really did despite how she treated him sometimes. It was

Heather that Jason sprinted towards though. She was helpless whereas Anne, he figured, could handle herself. Jason grabbed Heather as he reached her, dragging her along with him.

"Run, damn it! Run!" Jason yelled at Heather and she did, keeping up with him.

Jason glanced back over his shoulder to see Anne making her stand against the monster. She struck with her hatchet as the creature threw a punch at her. The hatchet's blade thunked into the knuckles of the clenched hairy hand coming towards her. It wasn't enough to stop the blow. Her hatchet embedded in the monster's hand and was torn from her grasp as Anne dove sideways, staying alive as the blow would likely have killed her outright. At that moment, Jason realized he had made a huge mistake leaving Anne on her own. He stopped, half turning to go back to help her but this time it was Heather who grabbed him.

"You can't help her, Jason!" Heather shrieked. "We're got to get out of here!"

In the heat of things, Jason's mind and emotions were too screwed up but do anything except listen to what Heather was telling him. He turned again and ran with her. As his legs pumped under him and his breaths came in ragged gasps, sweat slicking his skin, Jason heard Anne shout his name. His heart broke inside his chest as an instant later Anne cried out again, pain like he had never heard before in her voice. Jason knew she had just died. . .and there wasn't a damn thing he could do about it.

****

Dearil heard a woman die. He knew very well what a death scream sounded like and what he'd just heard was certainly that. The scream was somewhere just southwest of where he was. Curiosity and the desire to see her body got the better of Dearil, overriding his sense of self preservation. Abandoning his position where he had been considering eating a late lunch, Dearil darted through the trees, sprinting in the direction of the scream. Dearil had barely made it a quarter of a klick when a very sexy, young blonde woman in shorts and tank top half-covered by a denim jacket emerged from the trees ahead of him. Only his keenly honed, predator instincts kept him from putting a hole in her beautiful face as his pistol came up. His sharp eyes noted the man running along after her and the huge, hulking, hairy thing behind him. Adjusting his hand with a slight, fast bend of his wrist, Dearil fired twice. The man behind the blonde yelped as his bullets whizzed through the air, one on each side of his head. Dearil gawked in disbelief as the thing chasing the blonde and her friend launched itself to the right with impossible speed. He couldn't tell if either of his shots had even made contact with it. Dearil blinked in surprise. *I don't miss,* 1203122982 *he* wailed inside his mind, keeping his gun outstretched and ready.

"Don't shoot!" the blonde squealed.

"Get down!" Dearil shouted at the blonde and the man with her. Both of them dropped flat onto the ground.

Dearil had lost sight of the. . .whatever the hell it was but he could still hear it. The thing was bounding away from them. It was possible his shots had scared the thing off but Dearil doubted it. More likely, the creature was simply opting to wait for a better chance at taking them out or just wanted them to sweat awhile first, like him toying with his own prey.

Deep down, Dearil knew what he had just seen. The thing was a Sasquatch and a really ticked off one too. It had to be feral, a killer like himself, not the made up peaceful crap you often saw so called crypto-zoologists talking about on the TV. The tracks and bodies he had found at the campsite earlier in the day only added credence to the fact that his mind was still trying to deny. Bigfoot was real. . . and it was out here in these woods with them.

His attention was called back to the blonde and her friend.

"Mister!" the man shouted at him. "Mister, Anne is back there! We have to go back and help her!"

"Come on then," Dearil took a quick step to tower over the young man, extending a hand to help him up. The young man took it. Before he was on his feet though, Dearil struck with the butt of his pistol, smashing it into his forehead. The blonde cried out as the young man flopped back onto the ground, unconscious.

"Wha. . .?" the blonde stammered then wailed. "Why did you do that?"

Turning, Dearil pointed the barrel of his pistol directly at her. "I suggest you shut the hell up, girl."

"But that thing. . . it might come back," the blonde whimpered.

"It might," Dearil shrugged. "But we can't let that stop us from having some fun now, can we?"

His lips parted in a flashy smile. "Now, tell me, what's your name, girl?"

"I . . .I'm Heather and that's my friend Jason," she said through the sobs that shook her body. Tears ran down along the curves of her cheeks. Dearil could see just how confused she was by his actions. She was terrified with no idea of what was coming next. Dearil would have enjoyed it more if he knew whether the bulk of her fear was caused by him or the creature that his shots had hopefully driven off for a bit.

As much as Dearil would've liked to start playing with her then and there, he couldn't. Not without knowing where the Sasquatch had gone and if the beast really was coming back or not. Odds were it was. His gut told him the beast was playing its own game of horror with them just like he would do himself in its place. That meant they couldn't stay where they were. They needed to find somewhere safer. . . and doing so would be no easy task. This was the Sasquatch's home. It knew the land. They didn't.

Dearil went to work tying up Jason's hands with a belt from his backpack. He yanked it tight, making sure escape from it would be impossible as Heather watched him. She was still crying. It was a comforting sound that helped Dearil focus on the work at hand.

When he was content that Jason was bound well enough, Dearil stood up. "Your friend's going to be a pain in the arse to drag along with us. I'm not sure he's worth the effort."

"You can't just leave him! Please!" Heather begged.

Dearil savored the emotion coming out of her.

Of course, he had no intention of leaving the young man. Jason might come in useful after all.

"Get up!" Dearil ordered Heather. The blonde staggered to her feet. Heather's legs were shaky under her. She was fighting to just hold herself together and keep from losing it any more than she already had.

Taking a small knife from his pocket, Dearil squatted next to Jason knowing that Heather couldn't carry him and he sure as hell wasn't going to. He skewered Jason's right pointer finger with the blade, cutting into nerves there. Jason snapped awake, screaming, straining against the belt binding his hands. Dearil grabbed him by the hair on the back of his head.

"You keep struggling and you die!" Dearil warned.

Jason went still and then turned his head to get a better look at him.

"You're him, aren't you?" Jason rasped. "Dearil Horror?"

Dearil grinned. It was good to be recognized for one's work. He had always strived to make a name for himself. Dahmer, Darcy, all of them had nothing on him.

"I am," Dearil purred, watching Jason go pale.

"On your feet," Dearil barked.

Jason's hands were tied behind his back. Dearil

knew Jason had to be able to feel the blood pouring from the finger that he had torn up with his knife. It made him keep a smile on his lips despite the circumstances. Jason struggled onto his feet.

"Jason. . ." Heather said, starting towards him.

"Uh uh," Dearil waved the barrel of his pistol at her. "No getting closey."

Heather froze, waiting on him to tell her what to do next. Jason stayed where he was as well, smart enough apparently to know when to keep his mouth shut.

"We're heading north," Dearil told them. "You," he pointed at Jason, "take the lead but leave some distance between you and her."

Dearil followed after them allowing Jason to set the pace. He was only half paying attention to Jason and Heather, trusting that they were sufficiently scared to do what he said without giving him any problems. Instead, Dearil kept his focus on the woods around them, eyes scanning and ears listening for any sign of the Sasquatch. The beast could come at them at any moment and Dearil wasn't about to get caught with his guard down. One slip up and as fast and strong as the beast was, it'd be game over and his having fun would end forever.

"Hey!" Jason blurted out, stumbling into a wide clearing.

On him in an instant, Dearil shoved Jason onto his knees, left hand firmly grasping a shoulder to keep him there. It wasn't the Sasquatch that had caused Jason to freak out. It was what sat in the center in the clearing. From the looks of the place it was old. Vines grew up the sides of the cabin and the wood of its walls were worn by rain and time. Its door was partially open, swaying in the light wind that had kicked up while they were moving through the woods. It felt as if a storm was coming. The air was charged with an undefined energy.

There were two windows on its front side, one to each side of the main door. The left was intact but something had long ago shattered the right. Dearil motioned for Jason and Heather to remain where they were as he carefully approached the cabin's door. He took hold of the door and slowly opened it. The fading light of the day lit the interior. There was a bed on each side of the single room, a fireplace in the far wall, a table with two chairs in the room's center, and several cabinets lined the walls. Dearil gave a sharp nod of approval at the sight before him. It would do. If a storm was coming they would need shelter but he had no delusion that the place would keep them safe from the Sasquatch. That thing could tear through the door or even the walls easily.

Seeing that the cabin was clear, Dearil motioned for Heather and Jason to go in ahead of him. The air inside smelt of dust and rotting wood. Dearil waved a hand vainly in front of his face as if to chase away the odors.

"What is this place?" Heather asked, apparently working up the courage to speak to him. For a second, Dearil thought about slicing out her tongue. Not because she'd offended him or challenged his authority but simply for the fun of it. How beautifully Heather would writhe in pain with blood flowing over her lips but Dearil resisted the temptation. Instead, he decided to just answer her.

"Looks like this was somebody's getaway spot where good ole boys could come and do their huntin', I reckon," Dearil said in a mock Southern accent, laughing. "Don't suppose it matters. It's our new home for the time being now, kids."

Dearil pointed to the table. "Jason, if you'd be so kind as to have a seat over there."

The young man was beginning to get over his fear. Dearil could see that the desperation to find a chance to survive was growing in him. It wasn't at the point yet where something needed to be done about it but it likely would be sooner rather than later. Jason complied, taking a seat at the table.

"You, over there," Dearil directed Heather to the bed on the left side of the room.

She did what he said too but reluctantly. Her hesitation wasn't born of survival instinct like her friend's but rather disgust. The bed was gross. As Heather took a seat on it, a bug, that might've been a roach, skittered out of its mattress, dropping onto the floor and darting across it. Heather screamed, waving her hands about.

"Quiet!" Dearil barked and Heather settled down. Heather sat perfectly still, staring at him, terrified she was about to be punished for crying out.

Outside, a heavy rain began to fall. Dearil had always loved the sound of rain hitting a rooftop as a kid. He found it comforting now as well. There was some rope and chains piled up in a corner of the cabin. Dearil picked up a length of rope and used it to tie Jason to the chair he'd sat down in. Jason didn't resist him or even say anything. With a flick of his knife, Dearil cut off a portion of the rope and used it to bind Jason's feet together as well. Content with his work, Dearil smiled and turned his attention to seeing if there was anything in the cabin that might be of use to him. There was no food that was still edible. All of what was in the cabinets had spoiled some time ago. He did however find a pair of boots that actually fitted him and traded out his shoes for them.

"Now children, I don't know about you but I seriously need to get some rest," Dearil told Jason and Heather. "If either of you wake me or try to escape, I can promise you, there will be hell to pay."

Without another word, Dearil walked over and flopped onto the bed across from Heather's. It squeaked beneath his weight. Closing his eyes, Dearil relaxed and listened to the rain.

****

"This is Marshal Lucas to Sheriff Roland. Come in, over?" Lucas repeated a third time into his radio. The only response he got was still just static and crackling. Stephen was watching him with a frown on his face. Roland was supposed to have put together a larger group to hunt Dearil and be following after them as soon as he could. Without being able to reach the sheriff, Lucas had no idea what the status of that group was. He hoped it was on its way though. The discovery of the mauled black bear had left most of his own group on edge, including himself.

"You might as well give up, Marshal," Trevor told him. "These hills up here play devil with just about every kind of signal and that storm rolling in ain't helping nothing either. You ain't never gonna get him."

Lucas sighed, admitting defeat, and tucked away his radio.

"Anybody got a signal on their cell?" Stephen asked.

Everyone in the group shook their head in the negative as Trevor cackled.

"You don't listen very well, do ya?" the tracker asked Stephen.

"Shut up," Stephen warned, his frown turning to an angry snarl.

"That rain in the distance is moving in fast," Debra commented. The medic looked ready to pack it all in and head back. They couldn't do that though. Not while Dearil Horror was still on the loose.

"Any suggestions on what to do about that?" Stephen snapped at her.

Hedrick spoke up. "I think there's some cabins out here somewhere. Maybe we can locate one of them and hole up for a bit."

"Hey Trevor," Wolfman's deep voice rumbled. "You know where any of them are at?"

Trevor rolled his eyes. "Oh ye of so little faith that you need to ask."

"I'll take that as a yes," Arey said.

"Ain't none of them close enough to reach before that storm starts though," Trevor told them all and then spat a mouthful of tobacco juice into the grass at his feet. "And we're gonna need cover. There's been some pretty big lightning flashes and we don't wanna be in the open any longer than we have to."

"What are you suggesting?" Lucas asked.

"There's a cave a lot closer than them there cabins," Trevor answered. "I suggest we head for it and wait there for the storm to pass."

"You're the expert," Lucas said, nodding. "Lead the way."

"He called me an expert," Trevor cackled to Eliza.

"Oh brother," Eliza rolled her eyes. "Just get on with it."

With Trevor in the lead, the group got moving faster trying to reach their destination before the rain started. They didn't make it. The rain burst loose on them like a breaking dam. The downpour came hard and fast. Debra yelped as the cold drops poured over her. They were all soaked to the core as they reached the dark mouth of a cave that led into a hillside. Trevor stood at the opening, motioning for them all to hightail it inside. A roll of thunder boomed and a streak of lightning flashed in the sky as Lucas entered the cave last behind everyone else. The air was cold and damp but at least they were out of the rain and the wiping wind that had grown stronger over the last few minutes.

"You get a lot of weather like this?" Stephen asked Hedrick.

The lead deputy had slumped against a side of

the cave's mouth, just inside of it far enough for the rain not to hit him, and was checking over his AR-15. He looked up at Stephen with an annoyed expression. "Yeah. This time of year things can get dicey around these parts if you're not smart enough to be at home watching a game from the comfort of your recliner."

Lucas heard Arey stifle a giggle. The little woman had taken a seat next to Hedrick and leaned her sniper rifle up against the wall of the cave, her legs stretched out in front of her, clearly taking advantage of a chance to get some rest. He felt very much like doing the same. His legs were aching and his feet hurt.

"What's that smell?" Debra asked, disgusted.

"Sometimes bears and big cats use caves like this as homes for the winter," Trevor said and gestured towards the darkness of the cave's rear. "I wouldn't go too far back in there if I were you. Odds are you wouldn't like what you find."

"Great," Eliza shook her head.

"This storm should pass pretty quickly," Hedrick commented, "and then we can get back to it."

"If that was supposed to cheer me up," Eliza frowned, hugging one of her dogs to her. She'd brought all three of them into the cave with the group. "It doesn't."

The dogs were all keeping close to Eliza, looking

like they were the ones who needed comforting. The smallest of the three sat on its haunches, making whimpering noises.

"They don't like it in here any more than we do," Debra moved to begin petting the small dog.

"Shit," Wolfman huffed. "It ain't that bad."

"Says you, big guy," Stephen punched the huge deputy in the shoulder.

Lucas took charge of the situation, "Look, we're going to be stuck in here for a while so I suggest all of you get some rest."

"I got first watch," Hedrick said.

"Fine by me," Stephen assured the lead deputy, finding a place to sit down and stretch out. Stephen was asleep almost as quick as he closed his eyes.

Everyone but Lucas and Hedrick followed Stephen's example.

Hedrick had stopped messing around with his AR-15 and sat near the mouth of the cave staring out into the rain. Lucas walked over and took a seat opposite.

"First time you've had to track down someone in woods like these?" Hedrick asked.

"In woods this large," Lucas nodded.

"Figured," Hedrick smirked.

"The guide your sheriff stuck us with is insane," Lucas grinned, changing the subject somewhat.

"Trevor?   Can't argue that one," Hedrick shrugged. "I could say the same thing about your buddy over there."

Hedrick nodded at Stephen.

"Guy aimed his weapon at a fellow law enforcement officer," Hedrick said. "Ain't nothing right in the head about that."

"Yeah," Lucas admitted. "Sorry about that. He can be kind of hotheaded."

Gnawing on his lip and wishing he still smoked, Lucas turned his gaze out into the rain. The thick clouds had made the night come to the woods early. He couldn't see crap outside of the cave. If there was anyone or anything out there, they'd likely have to be right on top of him and Hedrick before either of them noticed.

"Your deputy, Arey, seems to believe what Trevor is preaching," Lucas said.

"I suppose that ain't a crime," Hedrick met his eyes. "You ask me, they're both crazy. Tell me, Marshal, do you believe in Bigfoot?"

Lucas didn't answer. Twenty-four hours ago, he'd have laughed outright at the idea. Today, he wasn't so sure. A feeling that something bad was going to happen had hung over him since the start of their manhunt for Horror. Finding a dead and partly eaten bear didn't help matters. Trevor hadn't pointed out the massive tracks around its corpse but

Lucas had noticed them. Maybe Deputy Arey had too. They were sure as hell something to think about. The tracks almost looked like they were left by a human foot except for the fact that they were so huge and deep. Whatever left them had to be heavy as it was tall.

"I didn't hear your answer," Hedrick quipped, still smirking.

Lucas sighed, seeing that the deputy wasn't going to let it go.

"I don't know," Lucas answered honestly.

Hedrick snorted. "That's what I thought. If you don't know better, Trevor can be pretty convincing."

"What makes you so sure he's wrong?" Lucas frowned.

"We're talking about Bigfoot, Marshal," Hedrick reminded him. "You ever seen one? No? Well, me either."

Outside, lightning flashed in the darkened sky and the rain continued to fall in waves.

****

Dearil woke up to the sound of snapping wood. He sat up on the bed, snatching the .30.06 he'd propped against it up from the floor, working the rifle's bolt to chamber a round. Jason had been trying to get loose from the chair that he was tied to and in the process broken part of its back. The young man froze like a deer in the headlights of an oncoming car at the sight of Dearil aiming the .30-.06 at him.

Clicking his tongue, Dearil stood up. "What did I tell you about trying to escape, kid?"

Jason didn't say anything. He just kept staring at the serial killer, sheer terror in his eyes.

"Please don't kill him!" Heather shouted. She'd been lying on the bed on the opposite side of the cabin from Dearil. Now, she sat up, hands clutching its edge so tightly next to her thighs that their knuckles were white.

The sight of her so helpless and upset made Heather all the more attractive to Dearil. Mentally chastising himself for losing focus, Dearil snapped at her. "Shut up, blondie!"

Dearil lashed out with the butt of his .30-.06, smashing it into Jason's face. There was a crunching sound as the young man's nose broke from the force of the blow and knocked him unconscious. Blood flowed from his nostrils as Jason slumped over in the chair.

"Jason!" Heather cried out.

"Girl!" Dearil spun on Heather. He sucked in a breath and forced himself to calm a bit. "I won't warn you about keeping your mouth shut again."

Dearil looked Heather over with greedy eyes. Things stirred within him. Perhaps it was time to have the fun he'd been waiting on. The storm outside was winding down and almost over and there was still no sign that whatever officers were dispatched to bring him in had any idea where he was. He took a step towards Heather where she was cowering on the cabin's other bed and froze. Somewhere outside, Dearil heard the Sasquatch roar. The sound of it chilled him to the bone. Dearil wasn't the sort to scare easily. It was a strange experience for him. Dearil was usually the alpha predator in most situations. Out there though was a beast unlike anything he'd ever encountered or even imagined could be real. He had seen the thing with his own eyes though and saw what it was capable of.

Heather's eyes were wide. She was even more terrified than before. That ticked Dearil off. She was supposed to be afraid of him, not some hair-covered giant outside. Nonetheless, Heather hadn't screamed at the sound of the beast's roar. Dearil smirked at that and tried to tell himself that he was still the monster of their story. He raised a hand signaling for Heather to stay where she was as Dearil crept towards one of the cabin's front facing windows. It had no rear ones.

Dearil wiped away grime from the glass with the

palm of his hand so that he could at least somewhat see outside. The cabin sat in the center of a clearing so if the Sasquatch came at it, there were no trees for it to creep through. Glancing left and then right through the window, Dearil couldn't see crap. The roar had sounded to be a hell of a lot closer than he would have liked. It put Dearil on edge. His gut told Dearil that the Sasquatch was done watching them and ready to get down to the bloody business of ripping them apart and making a meal of them. Dearil chuckled at that thought. He and the beast out there in the trees were very much alike in some ways. A small part of him was sad that he was going to have to find a way to kill the thing and send it back to whatever Hell it had crawled out of. The .30-.06 might have the power to stop the beast but his pistol sure didn't. Dearil still didn't know if he had hit the beast during their first encounter but if he had it had shrugged off the 9mm rounds as if they were nothing. Looking down at the rifle in his hands, Dearil figured even it would take more than one shot to down the beast. He weighed his odds of surviving a second encounter with the Sasquatch as not good at all. Soon he was going to have to make a choice - stay in the cabin or get on the move again. If he stayed, the cabin, in the center of the clearing surrounding it, gave him a better chance against the Sasquatch but staying meant the A-holes who were surely out there hunting for him had more of a chance of catching up to him. If he left though, it was going to be a hassle to bring Heather and Jason along, and he wasn't done with Heather yet, not to mention, he would be completely exposed, giving the Sasquatch the chance to take him off guard. . . and that would certainly be fatal.

Jason groaned where he sat, beginning to stir. Dearil sighed. His first plan had been to use the kid as bait for the Sasquatch but doing so had its own dangers. Dearil wondered if he should just go ahead and kill Jason, be done with it. He certainly wasn't going to drag Jason along if he decided to abandon the security of the cabin. Frustrated, Dearil slipped out a knife with his left hand, spun it with his fingers, and walked over to sink the blade into Jason's shoulder, twisting it there.

Howling in pain, Jason jerked and thrashed in the chair he was bound to. One of its legs finished snapping in two, sending the young man crashing to the floor. As Jason rolled about, Dearil started kicking him, over and over.

"Stop! Please stop!" Heather wailed but was thankfully smart enough not to leave the bed where he had told her to stay. That would have been too much of a violation and forced him to end her right then and there.

Jason went limp, blood flowing freely from his broken nose, lips, and several other spots on his battered face. Dearil kicked the young man a final time and towered above him, admiring the damage he had done with his boots. Their leather was drenched in a slick of warm red.

Heather was sobbing loudly but had listened to him about keeping her mouth shut. Dearil walked over to take her chin in his hand and raise her face up towards him. He looked into her eyes and smiled, feeling Heather shudder at his touch. Reluctantly releasing Heather, Dearil realized he hadn't heard the beast outside again. The Sasquatch had either fallen silent or left.

Dearil moved to the windows again, peering out one and then the other. There was no sign of the creature. He waited for several minutes, peering into the trees and listening, before finally deciding that the Sasquatch must have left. . .and that begged the question – why?

****

The storm had passed. Hedrick led the group out of the cave, heading north again. Lucas wondered just how large of a lead Horror had on them. He was surprised that they hadn't stumbled across some sign of the serial killer already. Dearil

Horror wasn't exactly known for his wilderness skills. Somehow though, he was clearly making it just fine through these woods and mountains.

Eliza had let her dogs loose. She hadn't wanted to but Stephen had pulled rank and left her no choice in the matter. Lucas could tell that his partner was beginning to get fed up with the whole situation. Stephen hated the outdoors and it showed.

The dogs were well out of sight of the group but they could still be heard, barking among the trees.

While Hedrick and Trevor were at the head of the group, Lucas, Stephen, Debra, and Eliza made up its center. Wolfman and Arey brought up the rear, both of the deputies keeping their eyes peeled in case Horror tried to come at them. There was no question that Horror was armed. The serial killer had taken a gun off the body of one of the marshals assigned to his transfer and had taken several blades from the diner as well. Lucas knew that Horror favored using blades for his kills but also knew that he was no idiot either. Dearil Horror would use anything and everything at his disposal to the best effect that he could in order to stay free. Horror was a damn smart bastard too. Still, so far they hadn't run into any traps left behind for them. That meant either Horror hadn't had the time to rig any up or that something else was likely keeping him occupied.

In the distance, the barking of the dogs hit a crescendo. They'd found something and from the sound of things engaged it. One of the dogs yelped loudly in pain and fell silent. Eliza was freaking out. She took off running, sprinting as fast as she could.

"Hey!" Hedrick shouted as she passed him and Trevor. "Hold up, damn it!"

Eliza wasn't listening though. She vanished into the trees.

"Frag it," Stephen grumbled and ran after her. The rest of the group followed.

None of them were prepared for what they were about to run into.

Another dog died in pain. From the sound of its cry, Eliza could tell her beloved animal was gone. As she burst from the trees into a small clearing, Eliza skidded to a halt, frozen by a primal instinct that rooted her where she stood with fear. Ahead of her was a monster like something out of a nightmare. The thing had to be a Sasquatch. It was a massive, thickly muscled beast covered in brown hair from head to toe with burning yellow eyes and stood around eight feet tall. It held the last of her dogs in one of its hands. Bone crunched and snapped as the thing broke the dog's neck and then flung its corpse away.

The others rushed into the clearing behind her.

"Holy frag!" Hedrick shouted, not believing his own eyes.

"What the hell is it?" Stephen blurted out.

"It's the Sasquatch!" Trevor yelped.

Lucas took charge, yelling, "Take it out!"

Wolfman and Lucas opened fire first. The big deputy's shotgun boomed in chorus with Lucas's. The beast staggered from the heavy slugs ripping into its torso and then quickly righted itself, charging straight at the group instead of running away. That took everyone by surprise, even Lucas. Hedrick tried to bring his AR-15 into play against the Sasquatch but it darted by him, knocking him aside like a discarded child's toy. Lucas jumped out of the creature's path as Wolfman stood his ground, unflinching. The big deputy looked small in comparison to the Sasquatch as it plowed into him like a linebacker. Wolfman's upper body was pushed backwards, his spine breaking with a sharp crack. Debra was screaming and running, sprinting away into the woods to the east, desperate to escape the monster's fury. Trevor died next. The little tracker was still staring at the Sasquatch he had fought to get folks to believe in for so long when one of its giant fists came down on his head. The bones of his skull were shattered as his head exploded like an over ripe melon being struck by a sledgehammer. Fragments of bone, brain matter, and blood flew everywhere. Trevor's headless body was still dropping to the ground as the Sasquatch kept moving onward through the group. Arey held her rifle leveled at the monster's chest but before she could get off a shot the hairy hand took hold of the weapon's barrel, yanking it upwards. The rifle cracked in the second before it was ripped roughly from her grasp. Arey's trigger finger went with the weapon. Blood spurted from where her finger had been attached as Arey howled in pain.

Stephen managed to get himself together enough to turn and take a shot at the monster that had just torn through their ranks and was darting away into the cover of the trees. His shotgun thundered but the round hit the trunk of a tree instead of the great beast. Chunks of splintering wood flew into the air. . . and then it was all over as fast as it had started. The Sasquatch was impossibly fast for something its size and was gone, disappeared into the woods, out of his sight.

"Medic!" Hedrick was shouting where he knelt next to Wolfman's body.

"Where the hell is that EMT?" Stephen barked as he spun to assess the causalities the group had taken.

"He's dead," Lucas said coldly to Hedrick and then turned his attention to where it might be able to do some good.

Eliza was still standing, stunned, and frozen by loss and fear. Lucas moved to take hold of her.

"You okay?" he asked, deep concern in his voice.

"My. . .my dogs," Eliza stammered in shock.

"A little help over here!" Arey cried out, holding her right hand with her left, blood pouring from where her missing finger had been.

Hedrick leapt to his feet. "Debra! Get your arse back here, woman!"

"Everyone calm down!" Lucas ordered.

Arey got up in his face. "Trevor and Wolfman are dead, I'm missing a damn finger, and our medic has run the hell off, Marshal! And you want us to calm down?"

Lucas hauled off and punched the short woman in the forehead. The blow knocked her out. She toppled over like a bag of bricks hitting the ground. He hated to do it but knew they all needed to get it together before the monster decided to come at them again.

"People!" Lucas shouted at the top of his lungs. "Calm the hell down and focus!"

"I hear ya, man," Hedrick answered, pulling himself together.

"Stephen, you and Hedrick go find Debra! Don't take any chances and make sure all of you come back alive!" Lucas barked at them. "Deputy

Arey, get over here and let me see that wound."

There was no need for him to say anything to Eliza. He could see that though she was lost in grief, the dog handler had at least woken up from her state of shock. Eliza moved to where the closest of her dogs lay, dead and broken in the grass, and dropped to her knees beside it.

The Sasquatch, if that was what it really was, had hit them so fast and hard, Lucas was barely holding it together himself. . . but someone had to.

****

Stephen and Hedrick moved quickly through the woods in the direction that Debra had run.

"Debra!" Hedrick bellowed.

No one answered him.

Stephen hadn't even remembered the EMT's name until he heard Hedrick shout it again.

Both of them were jerking their heads about, eyes scanning for any sign of the great beast that very well could still be around, ready to tear them apart limb by limb. By the look of the thing, Stephen knew the beast could do it too. The thing had taken out Wolfman like he was nothing and the deputy had been built like a professional wrestler.

"Hold up!" Hedrick cried out.

Stephen stopped, ready for anything, a round

chambered in his shotgun, his finger on the trigger.

"I found her," Hedrick told him.

Looking over to where the lead deputy stood, Stephen saw Debra huddled down in a bunch of bushes, whimpering, eyes wide with terror.

"It's okay," Hedrick reached out to touch Debra's shoulder. "That thing is gone now and we've got wounded who need you."

Debra allowed the lead deputy to help her onto her feet. "It's gone?"

"It's gone," Hedrick nodded.

"Did you kill it?" Debra asked.

Hedrick shook his head. "No, but we scared it off."

Stephen frowned at the lead deputy's lie but let it slide. They needed Debra's skill and if feeding her a load of crap got them it then so be it.

"We need to get back," the grumpy marshal urged Hedrick, eying the trees around them more nervously than he would ever admit.

"Come on," Hedrick helped Debra along. "We've got wounded who need you, Debra."

"I. . .I saw it kill Trevor and the big deputy, Wolfman," Debra stammered.

"It's Deputy Arey that's hurt," Hedrick informed her.

"Arey," Debra repeated the name as if it were an alien word. She was still badly rattled. Stephen just hoped Debra could get it together enough to do her job like she was supposed to.

They made it to where the others were waiting. Arey remained sprawled out on the ground, unconscious. Hedrick made a mental note that he was going to have to have some words with Marshal Lucas when this crap was over with; either that or file an official complaint against him. Nobody hit his people and got away with it. . . especially not Arey. As much as Hedrick loathed it, the short woman had a special spot in his heart. No one else knew it, not even Arey, but Hedrick thought the world of her. Arey was a fireball fury when she needed to be. He had seen her break up bar fights that would have given Wolfman pause wading into. As deputies went, Arey was one hell of a good one. Hedrick respected her a great deal. Maybe someday, Hedrick told himself, he might get the nerve to tell her what he thought of her.

Lucas had stripped Wolfman of his jacket and used it to partially cover the big deputy. He'd done the same for Trevor too. Eliza had gathered the bodies of her dead dogs and knelt next to them, weeping, body shaking with sobs. Hedrick felt her pain. Wolfman had been more than just a deputy to him. The big idiot had been a friend too.

Debra appeared to shake off the fear she was wrestling with, racing to where Arey lay.

Shrugging her pack from her shoulders, the EMT went to work, checking the unconscious deputy out and doing what she could for Arey's wound. Debra asked if anyone knew where Arey's missing finger was but no one did.

After giving Debra a few minutes, Lucas approached her. "She good?"

Debra nodded. "She'll be fine."

"Good," Lucas grunted. "Wake her up. We've got to get moving."

"Yes sir," Debra answered.

"Lucas," Stephen said, frowning again, "What are you thinking?"

"That thing. . ." Lucas shrugged. "It changes everything."

"No it doesn't," Stephen huffed. "That thing, whatever the hell it is, ain't the monster you're making it out to be right now in your head, Lucas. It's just an animal. A big and dangerous one, sure, but it's just an animal all the same. It can be killed if it has to be."

Scowling, Lucas sighed, "This is its turf, Stephen. It has all the advantages out here. . . and we're completely exposed."

"Not all the advantages, Lucas," Stephen tapped the side of his head. "Like I said, that thing is just an animal. We're a hell of a lot smarter than it is. If we're careful and keep our guard up, we can deal with it. Besides, I know you. You're not going to just walk away and let Dearil Horror make it out of here."

He and Stephen might be partners, even friends, but right now Lucas hated him for being right. Creature or no, Dearil had to be brought in before he could escape these woods into the world at large. If Dearil made it out, God only knew how many people would be tortured and die at his hands before anyone could catch up to him. Dearil was a smart enough killer to cover his tracks. Unless his time in prison made him careless, it could take months or even years to get Dearil in cuffs and back on his way to the execution that was waiting for him. If Dearil got away, it would be on him, at least in his own mind anyway. Lucas couldn't let Dearil loose on the world if there was any way at all to stop the killer. The Sasquatch, or whatever it was, well, it was something else altogether. Lucas had never even imagined something like it could really exist and the thing sure as heck wasn't something he was trained to deal with. It was his call whether they headed back or not.

"We need to radio Sheriff Roland," Lucas said. "Find out how close he is to making it out here with help."

"That's not gonna happen," Eliza said, getting up and turning her back on the bodies of her mangled dogs.

"Nope," Hedrick agreed. "We're too far away now. This place out here. . . it messes with signals, radio too, not just our cells."

Lucas tried using his radio anyway, "Come in, Sheriff. This is Marshal Lucas. Can you read me? Over."

The only answer he got was crackling static.

"Told ya, Marshal," Hedrick smirked. "You can keep wasting your time and breath if you want but ain't no one ever gonna answer ya."

Lucas threw his radio away in disgust. Keeping the anger born of his frustration in check as best he could, he said, "Do you know how to get to any of the cabins Trevor was taking us to?"

Hedrick nodded. "Yeah, I think so."

"Then that's where we're going," Lucas told them all. "We're too exposed out here."

"You heard him, Deputy," Stephen said. "Lead the way."

****

Dearil got brave enough to venture out of the cabin, fairly sure that the beast was gone for the time being. He was grateful to whatever might have drawn it away. Having tied up Heather before leaving and making sure that Jason was secured too in case the kid woke up, Dearil had no need to hurry in making his assessment of whether it was safe to get back on track with his original escape plan. Sadly, no matter what he did, there was just no means of knowing for sure without actually just rolling the dice.

He had halfway crossed the small clearing that surrounded the cabin when voices could be heard among the trees. Dearil froze, listening. There were several distinct voices, likely more than he could deal with, even ambushing them. Unable to hear them clearly enough to make out what was being said, Dearil figured his best course of action was to retreat into the cabin. It was possible whoever the people were, they were just passing by and had no idea the cabin was even here.

Hurrying back inside, Dearil was greeted with a wide eyed expression from Heather. She desperately wanted to ask him what was happening but knew better than to say anything. The corner of Dearil's lips ticked up in a partial grin at the sight of her bound to the bed she sat on with such emotion being directed at him.

Heather wasn't gagged so Dearil gave her a gentle reminder. "Not a sound out of you, girl, until I say otherwise. We've got company outside. One peep and I'll slice off your breasts. Nod if you understand that I ain't kidding."

Nodding frantically, Heather kept her mouth shut. Sitting helpless where she was, Heather watched Dearil peering out the cabin's right side window. Jason was still out cold, bound up, and lying on the floor. Dearil ignored them both, attention focused on those approaching outside.

A group of six emerged from the woods in front of the cabin. Dearil had dealt with enough marshals over his "career" to know that's exactly what two of them were. They were carrying Remington 870 shotguns. With them were a man and woman wearing sheriff department uniforms. The short, female deputy appeared to be injured. The other two of the six were a woman in an EMT uniform and a woman in plain clothes. Even Dearil's keen mind couldn't exactly place what the plain clothes woman might be. A guide, perhaps? Like the EMT, she wasn't armed other than a hatchet and knife that were sheathed on her belt. He'd been right about being unable to take on all of them by himself. He wouldn't have stood a chance alone out in the open. Holed up in the cabin though. . .that was another story. Dearil fetched his rifle and returned to stand beside the grimy window where he had been. If they decided to check out the cabin instead of turning away, the first shot at least would be his. Looking over his possible targets, Dearil figured his best bet was to drop one of the marshals before all hell broke loose as it surely would after he squeezed off that first shot.

Dearil held his fire, waiting to see what the group was going to do. They were only a threat if they opted to come into the cabin. The group stopped just outside the trees at the edge of the clearing surrounding the cabin. They were standing there talking among themselves as if trying to decide on what course of action to take. The marshal Dearil considered the largest threat was gesturing at the cabin, indicating the group was indeed going to cause him problems. The male deputy though looked to be arguing with the tough looking marshal. It was hard to tell who was winning their apparent argument. Dearil sighed. It was likely the marshal would pull rank on the deputy any second now.

Screw it, Dearil thought and then sprang into action. He fired through the grime covered window. It shattered, sending shards of glass flying. Heather screamed as the rifle cracked sharply. Outside, the high powered round Dearil fired entered the marshal's head on one side of his skull and exploded from its other side with a spray of bone fragments, blood, and brain matter following its wake. The marshal collapsed to the ground never knowing who or what killed him.

The male deputy and the remaining marshal

returned fire directed at the cabin at the same time. The deputy's AR-15 boomed in rapid succession. It was a semi-automatic weapon, but as fast as the deputy was pulling the trigger, that didn't matter. Round after round hammered into the cabin's wall and door. Both were too thick for the bullets to penetrate. The marshal however had discarded his shotgun, and drawn his pistol with the speed and skill of an Old West gunfighter. Dearil had to duck back as 9mm rounds came in through the window at him. One of them clipped his left arm, opening up a line of wet red across it just below his shoulder.

"Frag it!" Dearil snapped. Ignoring the pain of his wound, he followed the marshal's example, tossing the bolt action rifle aside. It thudded onto the floor as Dearil switched to using his Glock. Its higher rate of fire was what he needed. When the barrage of rounds striking the cabin and coming through the window came to a stop, Dearil leaned back around to see that the group outside had scattered. Some of them were running for cover while the others were in the process of reloading. Dearil popped off a series of shots at the male deputy and remaining marshal. He didn't take the time to aim so none of them hit. The shots were merely meant to keep the group outside from advancing on the cabin and hopefully drive them back. If he could force them to hold off until back up came, Dearil knew he might be able to escape whereas right now he was trapped with no way out at all. Dearil had no intention of dying inside a mess of rotting wood and dust.

****

Lucas's Glock barked repeatedly as he fired another burst of rounds at the window where Dearil was. Everything had gone to crap so fragging fast, Dearil had them on the defensive. A glance at Stephen's corpse made Lucas feel sick to his stomach. His friend's brains were splattered in the grass of the clearing and what was left inside Stephen's skull was slowly leaking out.

"Hey!" Hedrick shouted at him. "We gotta fall back, man!"

Lucas couldn't argue with him. He knew what a good shot Dearil was supposed to be despite the serial killer's rep for favoring blades. If they didn't get to better cover, even with the amount of fire they were pouring into the cabin to keep Dearil behind cover, he would eventually get lucky and nail one of them.

"Head for the trees!" Lucas jumped up from where he crouched, legs pumping under him as he ran for cover. He and Hedrick zigged and zagged their way to the tree line. Surprisingly, Dearil didn't take the chance to peg one of them in the back. Likely, Dearil was reloading. They couldn't be lucky enough for the bastard to have run out of ammo.

Eliza, Debra, and Arey were waiting for them there. Arey's expression was grim. She had her Glock drawn, hefting it in her left hand.

"Ain't no way we can get him in there without paying heavily for it, Marshal," Arey told Lucas.

"She's right," Hedrick grunted.

"So what do we do?" Eliza asked.

"We should be getting the hell out of these woods!" Debra blurted out.

"Shut up!" Lucas snapped at the EMT. He was still mentally reeling from the loss of Stephen. "Just give me a moment, damn it."

"That was a .30-.06 he took out your partner with," Hedrick said. "And he has a Glock too. The question, I guess, is how much ammo does he have for those weapons?"

"Does it matter?" Debra squealed. "You guys go at the cabin again and he will take you out."

"He can't holdout in there forever," Eliza said. "When Sheriff Roland and the big group he was putting together gets here, I am sure some S.W.A.T. guys can storm the place or something."

"Something's happening!" Debra pointed at the cabin. "Look!"

The door opened but it wasn't Dearil who was standing there. It was a young, blonde girl that looked as if she'd been put through Hell.

"He says keep away or he'll kill us!" the young blonde wailed and then just as suddenly as the door opened, it slammed shut.

"Frag me," Hedrick shook his head. "He's got hostages in there. How the hell did that happen?"

"Must be hikers or campers he stumbled across," Eliza frowned.

"That's just all the more reason for us to get out of here while we can," Debra urged. "We need help with him, help against that monster. If it comes back. . ."

"Debra," Eliza reached out to touch the EMT on her shoulder. The contact was meant to calm Debra down but all it did was stir her up more. The EMT slapped Eliza's hand away.

"We need to leave. Now!" Debra spat.

Deputy Arey leaned into Debra's face. "Shut your face and calm the hell down or I will fragging sedate you with your own gear."

The venom in Arey's eyes had the desired effect where Lucas's words had failed. Debra's lips snapped closed and she sat staring at Arey with fear in her eyes.

Lucas had been thinking while Debra had carried on before Arey finally silenced her. He'd come up with a plan. It wasn't a great one but it was a plan.

"Okay, people," Lucas spoke up. "We're not going anywhere without Dearil."

Hedrick grunted. "Marshal. . ."

"We don't have to get into that cabin, Deputy Hedrick," Lucas said. "All we have to do is get Dearil to come out."

Hedrick's eyes widened showing that the deputy clearly hadn't gone down that road of thinking. "And how the hell do we manage that?"

Lucas just grinned. Dearil was too smart to ever believe that they'd just leave and let him be.

"We just need to get to Stephen's body," Lucas told the lead deputy.

"What? Why?" Hedrick asked.

"He brought a tear gas along," Lucas smiled. "We get that, either Dearil will come out or we can rush him with a hell of a lot less risk."

"For fragging sure," Hedrick agreed, "But who is going to go out there and get it?"

"I will," Arey said before Lucas could answer.

"Whoa now," Hedrick protested.

"I'm small and I am fast," Arey pointed out. "If you guys can just give me some cover, I can get it. No worries."

"We can do that," Lucas promised. "But don't make a move until we start shooting. Got it?"

"Got it," Arey nodded.

Hedrick was fuming. Lucas saw that the lead deputy had more than professional feelings for Arey. . . but she was the best choice for the job that needed doing and Arey wanted to do it. Hedrick was trying to keep his feelings out of it, at least enough not to argue anymore. The lead deputy was grimly accepting the cards that fate had dealt them.

****

"Dearil!" Lucas yelled from the cover of the trees. "What say we talk this through?"

No answer came from the cabin.

"You might as well talk, Dearil," Lucas carried on. "We both know I am not going anywhere without you in cuffs ahead of me."

"I have two kids in here with me, Marshal," Dearil shouted back. "You come at this place and they'll pay for your bravado with their lives."

"Tell you what, Dearil. . ." Lucas called out. "You leave them in there and come out on your own, I give you my word I'll let you have a five minute head start before we come after you."

Lucas heard Dearil cackling.

"You must think I'm an idiot, Marshal," Dearil answered. "I open this door without one of the kids in front of me and I'm dead."

"What are you hoping to accomplish by this?"

Hedrick whispered to Lucas. Lucas motioned for the lead deputy to hush.

"You don't trust me? I said I'd give you my word," Lucas responded.

"I'll give you that you are very amusing, Marshal," Dearil was still laughing. "What's your name?"

"You can call me Lucas."

"Well, Marshal Lucas," Dearil's voice came through the shattered window of the cabin. "I have a counter offer. You all come out of those trees, lay your weapons on the ground, and I'll not only let the kids go but I'll leave you all here to do whatever you like."

"This is getting us nowhere," Arey snarled from behind Lucas and Hedrick.

Lucas sensed that she was on the verge of taking matters into her own hands too late. As he turned to Arey, the little deputy bolted by him. Lucas made a grab at her but missed. Spinning back around, he brought up his Glock. Hedrick saw him and understood. The time to make their move was on them whether they were ready or not.

Arey burst from the trees, sprinting across the clearing towards Stephen's corpse. Hedrick opened fire with his AR-15 as Lucas started shooting his Glock.

"Frag!" they heard Dearil cry out from inside the

cabin.

Sliding like a baseball player trying to steal home base, Arey reached Stephen's body. The little deputy's hands slapped on his body, feeling around his pockets for the tear gas grenade he was supposed to be carrying. A cacophony of gunfire continued to roar as Lucas and Hedrick attempted to keep Dearil pinned down and unable to take a shot at her. The palm of her right hand felt a bulging mass. Reaching in to where it was, Arey pulled out a sleek, thin canister – the tear gas grenade. Arey rolled away from Stephen's corpse, springing to her feet. She ran for the cabin, attempting to keep out of the others' line of fire.

"What the frag is she doing?" Lucas barked at Hedrick.

"She's being herself," Hedrick quipped.

Arey had nerve, a hell of a lot of it, Lucas thought. No wonder Hedrick had feelings for the short deputy.

Hedrick's rate of fire with his AR-15 picked up, his bullets blasting to bits sections of the cabin's wall around the window where they'd last seen Dearil.

Reaching the cabin, Arey threw herself flat against its wall near the left window as Dearil suddenly began to return fire out of it. The serial killer's Glock cracked in rapid succession. Arey knew it was now or never. Flinging the grenade through the window at Dearil, she hurled herself away from the wall, racing around the corner of the cabin.

Inside, the grenade hissed, expelling its contents after landing on the wooden floor. It spun around as a cloud of tear gas filled the cabin.

****

"Damn it!" Dearil raged as tear gas stung his eyes and nostrils. He jerked the upper part of his shirt to cover his face with it. His first thought was to grab the grenade and fling it out the window. The A hole with the AR had paused to reload and was shooting at him again with a fresh mag. Dearil couldn't chance going near the window. Turning, he aimed his Glock at Jason and put a bullet into the young man's head. That was one problem solved at least. Heather was wailing like a dying cat. He'd been exposed to tear gas before. She never had. First times, in Dearil's opinion, usually were the worst for most things and tear gas was no exception to that rule of life. Rushing to the cabin's sink, Dearil discovered there was no running water. He was screwed, not that it would have really saved him anyway.

"You killed him!" Heather rasped, trying to

breathe and in a staggering amount of pain from the gas. It was a wonder the girl could even still see anything that was happening.

Cursing his luck, Dearil knew there was only one thing he could do.

"Marshal Lucas!" Dearil shouted. "Hold your fire! I'm surrendering!"

"I'll believe it when I see it, Dearil!" he heard the marshal yell.

Throwing open the door to the cabin but making damn sure not to be in the doorway, Dearil threw his Glock out the door and then chucked his rifle after it. He was coughing, lungs burning like hell. The girl, Heather, was in even worse shape. Dearil moved to the bed, cutting her loose, and shoved Heather towards the door. She staggered through it without being ripped apart by a barrage of fire from those outside. Dearil hoped it would go as well for him as he followed after her.

Heather had collapsed on the ground, unmoving, as Dearil staggered out, nearly tripping over her. Dearil's hands were raised above his head. "I'm unarmed!"

"Bull!" Lucas screamed back at him. "Drop the damn knife, Dearil!"

Dearil complied. He'd forgotten about the knife clutched in his right hand. Dearil flung it aside, making sure the marshal and his people could see that it wasn't aimed in their direction.

"On the ground!" a voice that didn't belong to the marshal ordered. "Hands on your head!"

Dropping to his knees, Dearil clasped his hands together behind his head, still fighting against the pain of the tear gas despite now being in the fresh air. Several people came out of the woods; one in the uniform of an EMT, rushed to the girl, rolling her over to pour either water or saline, Dearil couldn't tell, into her eyes. He was blinking himself, his vision blurred from the harm the gas had done.

The marshal, Lucas, ran up to Dearil, grabbing his hands roughly to slap cuffs on them. Dearil couldn't have resisted even if he wasn't still suffering from the tear gas exposure. The male deputy had the barrel of an AR-15 aimed at his head. Dearil didn't doubt that the deputy would blow his brains out if he so much as flinched the wrong way.

"What's your name?" Debra asked the young girl who had been Dearil's hostage.

"Heather," the young girl stammered.

"It's okay, Heather," Debra told her, "You're safe now. No one's going to hurt you anymore."

Somewhere in the distance, beyond the clearing around the cabin, the Sasquatch roared.

"Oh frag," the deputy covering him with the AR muttered.

"Is that thing coming this way?" the EMT shouted from where she was tending to Heather.

Dearil couldn't see Lucas. The marshal was behind him. He heard his voice though.

"Everybody keep your eyes on the trees!" Lucas ordered.

Dearil was laughing. He couldn't help himself.

"Oh it's coming, Marshal," Dearil promised, knowing that a confrontation with the great beast was coming no matter what any of them did. This was the beast's home and they were the intruders. It wasn't going to let them go without making them pay for violating its turf. The beast had their scent and they would feel its vengeance. Dearil knew that in his bones, one killer understanding the mind of another. And the beast certainly was a killer. He'd seen its handiwork with his own eyes. The marshal and his people had just gassed their only partly secure place to retreat to. "And when it gets here, there won't be any stopping it. You and your people will bleed."

"So will you," the marshal snapped at him.

"What do we do?" the woman in civilian clothes asked.

"We can't go in the cabin, Eliza. That's not an option now," the deputy with the AR pointed at him pointed out.

Dearil started laughing again. "You screwed

that up nicely, didn't you, Marshal?"

"On your feet," Lucas barked, jerking him up. Dearil staggered a bit but quickly found his balance despite the effects of the gas and the cuffs binding his hands behind his back.

"I do so like it rough, Lucas," Dearil purred.

Lucas didn't rise to his bait, ignoring the comment. That impressed Dearil. This Lucas truly seemed to have his head together.

"Everybody form up," Lucas said. "Hedrick, I want you in the lead. Arey, you got the rear."

"We're moving out?" Eliza asked.

"No choice," Lucas told her. "We're heading back to meet up with the sheriff."

"Yeah, he should be on his way by now," Hedrick nodded.

"Debra, that girl. . ." Lucas looked at the EMT.

"She's a little roughed up but fine," Debra answered.

"Alright people," Lucas jerked at Dearil's cuffs roughly again. "Let's get moving."

Another roar rang out from somewhere to the west of their location. Dearil marched in front of Lucas. He wanted to test his cuffs, confident that given a few seconds, escape from them would be possible, but didn't try them. It was obvious that he wouldn't make it more than a few yards at best before the marshal or one of the deputies put a round in his back.

****

Lucas watched Dearil closely. He knew that even in cuffs the serial killer was still dangerous as hell. The group was moving fast, maybe too fast. Lucas didn't dare call out for Hedrick to slow down. The beast, be it a Sasquatch, demon from Hell, or whatever, from the sound of its cries was drawing closer to them.

There was no further warning before the hulking, hair-covered monster charged into the middle of the group. Lucas was stunned. It hadn't sounded *that* close. Just how fast was the thing?

Over-sized hands reached out, taking hold of Dearil. The serial killer was lifted effortlessly from the ground, feet kicking wildly about in the air. Mouth opening wide, the great beast sunk its teeth into the top of Dearil's head. There was a crunch of bone as the teeth broke through to send blood and cerebral fluids splattering. Dearil's body twisted about frantically in the beast's grasp and then went limp. The serial killer hadn't even had the time to scream as he died.

Lucas snapped out of his shock, bringing his pistol up towards the giant creature. A burst of semi-automatic fire from an AR-15 struck the creature in the side before Lucas could squeeze the pistol's trigger. Grunting in pain, the monster spun and charged at Hedrick.

Taking a quick look around, Lucas saw that the group had broken up. Eliza was running east with Arey on her heels as if trying to stop the dog handler. The young girl, Heather, and Debra had split off to the west. There wasn't a damn thing he could do about it.

Hedrick's AR-15 boomed in rapid succession as the lead deputy poured rounds into the hulking beast that was coming at him like a runaway freight train. Each bullet thudded home in the Sasquatch's chest. Lucas couldn't deny what it was any longer. The thing had to be a Sasquatch. There was nothing else it could be. The rounds hitting the Sasquatch weren't really doing more than drawing a bit of blood and enraging the beast more than it already was. The thing's muscles were so thick and dense that the bullets weren't getting any real penetration. Lucas realized that if he didn't do something, Hedrick was about to die.

"Hey! Ugly!" Lucas yelled, chasing after the Sasquatch, his pistol cracking as he ran. "Over here!"

One of his shots slammed into the rear of the Sasquatch's skull. That got its attention though the 9mm round didn't do anything more than likely sting the creature. The Sasquatch spun about. Lucas looked straight into its eyes. They burned with rage and primal fury. Lucas's instincts pushed him to run like Hell but he held his ground, shifting into a two handed firing position to better his aim. As the Sasquatch raged, black lips parted into a bestial snarl, Lucas took his shoot. A 9mm round punched into the Sasquatch's left eye. Pulp and goo exploded outward as the bullet entered. The Sasquatch shrieked in sudden, unexpected pain, stopping in its path, raising its hands to cover its face. Blood ran through the fingers of its hair-covered hands. Lucas lowered his aim, putting another three rounds into the monster's chest despite knowing that they wouldn't do much. The Sasquatch was swinging its head around, hands still clasped over its face, as Lucas finally bolted into the trees. He'd lost sight of Hedrick. The lead deputy had made a run for it too.

Lucas hadn't paid attention to which way he had bolted, quickly realizing he had run in the same direction that Eliza and Arey had gone. He caught a glimpse of the two women through the trees and pushed himself onward harder in an attempt to catch up to them.

Arey, glancing over her shoulder, saw him coming. She didn't slow down though. The little deputy kept her pace, still trying to overtake Eliza.

The dog handler was a lot better at navigating the woods than either of them and that was clear just watching her, the way she weaved and zagged, dodging low tree limbs and not getting tripped up by roots that protruded up through the earth. Though somewhat separated, the three kept running for several minutes before Eliza skidded to a halt, Arey nearly crashing into her. Lucas emerged from the trees in their wake.

Before them was another cabin. Unlike the one they had found Dearil in, this one wasn't rickety, rotting, and on the verge of giving in to the elements. This cabin was fairly newly built and appeared to have been used not too long ago. Trevor had told them there were several cabins in the area and Lucas was grateful that they had managed to stumble onto another one. The place could very likely save their lives.

"Try the door," Arey snapped at Eliza.

The dog handler rushed forward to do just that. It was locked. Peering through the front window though, Eliza could see that the cabin was devoid of inhabitants.

Turning to the others, Eliza said, "It's locked."

"Let me at it," Arey hurried to shove Eliza aside.

Lucas watched, amused, as Arey went to work picking the cabin's lock. In less than a minute, the little deputy had the door open and was motioning for him and Eliza to get inside. Arey closed up behind them, relocking the door.

The cabin's interior consisted of a large main room that served as living space, bedroom, and kitchen with a small table but there was also an adjoining bath. Everything was modern, or close to it. Arey tested the water in the sink while Eliza flicked a light switch to see if there was power. The water ran but the light didn't come on.

"There has to be a generator somewhere," Arey commented.

"I bet it's out back," Lucas said. "We don't really need it though. The noise would only draw that beast here anyway."

"Good point," Eliza agreed.

"Did you see what happened to the others?" Arey asked Lucas.

He knew she was concerned about Hedrick. Wishing he had a better answer for her, Lucas answered, "No. I lost sight of him."

"We need to go back," Arey said, "The others might still be alive."

"There's no way to know that," Lucas shrugged. "And even if they were, we're in no shape to be of any use to them."

"Lucas is right, Arey," Eliza tried to keep from sounding cold. "We have to stay here. It's our only shot at getting out of these woods alive."

"You do what you want," Arey snarled, starting for the door, "I am not leaving them out there to die and be eaten by that. . .that thing!"

Lucas stepped in her path, blocking Arey from leaving. "I can't let you do that, Deputy."

"Get out of my way, Marshal," Arey tried to get by him but Lucas wasn't moving.

"Stand down, Deputy," Lucas barked. "That's an order."

"I don't take orders from you, sir," Arey argued.

"Listen to him," Eliza pleaded, tears welling up in her eyes. "If you go out there you'll die."

Eliza's desperation to stop her made Arey stop and think. The little deputy swallowed hard. Lucas saw that Arey was fighting not to cry herself.

Arey nodded slowly and backed away from the door. Without saying another word, she took a seat at the cabin's table and started checking over her Glock to make sure the pistol would be ready if it was needed. She had lost her rifle along with the trigger finger of her right hand during the group's first encounter with the Sasquatch.

Moving close to Lucas, Eliza whispered, "Do you think she's going to be okay?"

"She has to be," Lucas whispered back.

****

Lucas's attack on the Sasquatch had saved Hedrick's life. Hedrick owed the marshal if they survived the nightmare they were trapped in out here in these woods. When the Sasquatch turned on the marshal, Hedrick had used the distraction Lucas provided for him to take off after Debra and the young girl, Heather. He had caught up with them and now the three marched together through the trees. All of them were exhausted and waiting for the Sasquatch to come after them again.

Hedrick didn't dare head back in the direction he had last seen Lucas and the Sasquatch. He was the only protection Debra and Heather had. Neither of the women were armed. Not knowing where the Sasquatch had gone was a problem. It wasn't a certainty that the great beast had truly gone after Lucas. For all Hedrick knew the beast might be after them right now. Sometimes animals like to play with their prey and a beast as cunning as the Sasquatch might well be into that sort of thing.

"Do you think we lost it?" Debra asked.

"That was the thing that killed my boyfriend!" Heather said, gasping for breath, sweat dripping from her.

"What?" Hedrick questioned her. "I thought Dearil. . ."

"No! That nutjob got my friend Jason and I after that thing attacked us," Heather explained.

"Frag," Hedrick shook his head. Just how many people had the beast killed? It was looking like Trevor and Arey were right about it. The thing had likely been lurking in these woods, tearing folks apart its entire life and only God knew how long that was. "We've got to get out of these woods."

"That's what I have been saying," Debra reminded the deputy.

"Hush!" Heather quieted them. "Did you hear that?"

The trio went silent, all listening to the woods around them. At first, the sound was distant but it was growing closer with each passing heartbeat. Something huge was tearing through the woods in their direction. Tree branches were snapping and Hedrick's increasing fear almost made it feel like the ground itself was shaking beneath his feet. He held himself together though, readying his AR-15.

"Either of you ever use a gun before?" Hedrick barked at Heather and Debra.

"I have," Heather yelled back at him.

"Here!" Hedrick drew his sidearm and threw it to the young girl.

Heather caught the pistol and worked its slide, chambering a round. Hedrick was impressed by how she handled the Glock. He wondered who had taught her.

Hedrick was still trying to decide whether to tell

the girls to run for it or they should all try to make a stand and hold their ground when the Sasquatch came bursting from the trees. The beast let out a roar so loud it hurt Hedrick's ears. The deputy jerked his AR-15 up, opening fire. Bullets ripped at the Sasquatch's body, thudding into the muscles of its chest and arms. Heather was firing too, her Glock cracking over and over. The barrage of rounds hitting the Sasquatch didn't stop it though. The beast closed on him with inhuman speed. One of its large, hair-covered hands tore Hedrick's rifle from his grasp and flung the weapon away into the trees. The other closed around his neck. Hedrick would have met his death right then and there, he knew, if it wasn't for Heather. The young girl started shooting upwards, putting two point blank rounds into the side of the Sasquatch's head. The Sasquatch let go of him. Hedrick fell onto the ground at its feet as the beast whirled on Heather. Scrambling to his feet, Hedrick retreated, glancing helplessly over his shoulder to see the Sasquatch take hold of Heather, thick fingers breaking through the bone of her skull, sinking into her head. Then, with a single tug, its hands ripped Heather's head apart. An explosion of gore covered the beast, drenching its hair with a hot, wet red.

"No!" Hedrick screamed but Heather was already dead.

In an utterly unexpected show of courage, Debra threw herself onto the hulking monster's back. The EMT had a scalpel she used like a knife, plunging it into the Sasquatch's throat. The blade wasn't long enough to really open anything up but nonetheless drew blood. The Sasquatch shook, flinging Debra off of it. Now weaponless, Hedrick could only watch as the Sasquatch focused its fury on her.

Debra skittered backwards on the ground trying to escape its rage but the Sasquatch reached to pick her up. A booted foot slammed into the beast's groin as Debra continued to fight back. The Sasquatch smashed Debra into the ground then swung her body upwards like a child's toy, bringing it down again, over and over. Each impact was more sickening than the last. Blood flew and bones broke until Debra's leg finally came loose from her body. The Sasquatch stood, looking at the leg it held as if puzzled that she had come apart so easily.

Hedrick ran for his life. The girls were dead. All that mattered now was making it out of the woods alive so that he could let the world know about the monster that lived out here. Somebody had to stop the thing or it would just keep killing anyone and everybody that came across its path in these woods.

The beast was chasing him. Hedrick heard the monster drawing closer. He was pushing himself to his limits and beyond but it was still gaining on him. Fear kept him from glancing over his shoulder to see just how close the beast was. Hedrick zagged to the left and then darted around the trunk of a tree to the right. His only advantage was being smaller than the hulking Sasquatch. He was desperately trying to use it to stay ahead of the monster, keeping the trees between them.

Hedrick heard the Sasquatch change course then suddenly it was in front of him, appearing out of nowhere. Unable to stop, Hedrick ran straight into the monster, bouncing off of it. Before he could recover his balance and right himself, the Sasquatch's arms closed about him. Hedrick tried to scream but his ribs folded inward, impaling his lungs inside his chest. As his mouth opened, it was a geyser of blood that came out instead of a scream. He died almost instantly, feeling a sharp pain before his world went black.

****

Lucas stood at the cabin's window, peering out at the trees. So far, there had been no sign of the Sasquatch. Arey still sat at the table where she'd taken a seat after they'd found the place. Her expression was a mixture of grimness and loss. Eliza walked over to place a hand gently on his shoulder.

"It's getting late," the dog handler told him.

"I was hoping Sheriff Roland would have stumbled onto us by now," Lucas sighed.

"Still can't reach him on the radio?" Eliza frowned. "I knew signals didn't work well out here but I was hoping. . ."

"We're on our own," Arey huffed. "The sooner you two realize that, the better."

The little deputy had grown harder and darker since the group had lost Hedrick. They didn't know for sure if he was dead or just out there somewhere, waiting on help just like they were. Arey was apparently assuming the worst. Her chair creaked, skidding over the wooden floor of the cabin as she got up.

"We need to secure this place before it gets dark," Arey said.

"Arey. . ." Eliza started.

"Stop," Arey snapped. "Just stop it. I've got it together now and you two need to get your heads back in the game too. We can't just sit here waiting for that monster to come and find us. We need to be getting ready for it. A good start would be getting a fire going in the fireplace over there. The generator is too loud to risk but a fire. . .that has enough uses to make it worth taking a chance on."

Eliza nodded and rushed to try to get one going.

"We'll need to cover this window," Lucas commented.

"And board it up too," Arey added. "Got any thoughts on the door?"

"Nothing in here we could brace against it is going to keep that monster out," Lucas told her. "That thing is just too strong. If it really wants in here, it's getting in no matter what we do."

"Can the negativity, Marshal," Arey scowled at him. "You're right but that doesn't mean slowing the thing down wouldn't be a good idea."

"Sure," Lucas admitted.

The trio went to work. With some effort, Eliza got a fire going. Lucas used the tablecloth as a heavier blind for the window and then he and Arey scooted the table over, flipping it up onto its side against the door, and then nailed it in place. At that point, the three of them worked together as quickly as they could to board up the window, leaving small spaces between the bits of wood they used so that they could still see outside if they needed to.

There was warm beer in the fridge. God only knew how long it had been in there. Lucas didn't care. Beer didn't normally go bad. Temperature and time mainly only affected the taste. He popped the can open and took a swig. Yep, tasted like crap but Lucas didn't care. When he was younger, he'd drunk enough Bud to know that no matter how bad beer tasted, eventually you just didn't care. It still got you drunk. He wasn't looking to get drunk right now. That would be stupid. But he could use something to take the edge off of his nerves.

"Drinking on duty?" Eliza teased.

"Just trying to stay alive," Lucas grinned at her.

"I think that's everything we can do in terms of making this place safe," Arey said, placing the last chair from the table facing towards the barricaded door. The others had been broken up for wood either for the fire or to board up the window.

Lucas, beer in hand, walked to the window and carefully pushed aside its covering in a space between the boards nailed over it and looked outside. Night had fallen. The woods were dark and deep pools of black existed among the trees. Lucas couldn't see much. There didn't appear to be any sign of the Sasquatch outside though.

"I'll take first watch," Arey announced.

"No," Lucas turned from the window to face the little deputy. "You're going to get some rest."

"You pulling rank on me again?" Arey looked on the verge of coming at him.

Lucas shook his head. "Not at all, Deputy but you were hurt today. Look at your hand. That bandage needs to be changed and you need some rest."

"Here," Eliza jumped in. "Let me help.

There's a first aid kit in the bathroom."

Arey didn't argue. She let Eliza lead her away to treat her wound.

Lucas turned back to the window. He ran the fingers of his left hand through his hair. It was a nervous tick of his that helped Lucas focus. Part of him was still in denial that Stephen was dead. Dearil too. The man they had risked their lives in order to bring to justice and stop from killing again had stumbled into a fate that he deserved. Monster had slain monster right before Lucas's eyes. Taking another swig from his beer, Lucas let the cloth fall back into place over the window and looked around the cabin. The fire was crackling in the fireplace. He was alone in the main room. Eliza and Arey were in the adjoining bath. Mentally taking stock of what weapons that they had left, Lucas wondered if they would be enough. He still had his shotgun and sidearm. Arey only had her Glock. Eliza had nothing. They had searched around the cabin for other weapons but there wasn't anything in terms of other guns or ammo. There had been an axe, which Eliza claimed. Lucas supposed the axe was better than nothing if the Sasquatch made it inside. Of course, if the thing got that close to them again, they were likely all dead. If and when the beast showed itself, their only real hope was to take it down before they were forced into melee combat with it.

Eliza and Arey emerged from the bathroom.

"That feels better, doesn't it?" Eliza asked.

Arey nodded, glancing down at the clean bandage on her hand. The little deputy headed for one of the cabin's two beds and crawled onto it. Stretching out, she closed her eyes and listened to Lucas in trying to get some rest.

"You should get some rest too," Lucas told Eliza.

"Yeah, sure," Eliza answered indifferently.

"Eliza. . ." Lucas stared at her.

She wandered over to the window, carefully looking outside.

"I don't know how anyone can sleep with that thing out there," Eliza frowned.

"Deputy Arey appears to be managing it just fine," Lucas chuckled softly.

Eliza let the cloth fall back over the window behind the boards, turning to face him. "Well, I'm not her."

Tears welled up in her eyes all of a sudden. "That thing tore my world to shreds."

Lucas knew she was talking about her dogs. Nobody could have processed a loss like that in so short a time, especially not while fighting for their own life.

"I am sorry about your dogs," Lucas told her.

"Me too." She shook her head.

The window broke behind them. The boards covering it were shattered, splintering, and knocked aside. It wasn't giant, hair-covered hands that came through into the cabin but rather the end of a broken tree limb. Lucas watched the end of the limb explode outward from the center of Eliza's chest, impaling her. Her warm, wet blood splattered over him. Lucas blinked in shock as Eliza toppled over onto the cabin's floor.

"Eliza!" Lucas yelled, leaping up from the chair facing the door.

Arey jerked awake, rolling off her bed. Instinctively, she grabbed up her pistol with her trigger fingerless right hand and was forced to switch it to her left. "What the hell is going on?!?"

"Eliza's down," Lucas barked. "Help her!"

Lucas moved to the window, his shotgun booming, firing a shotgun blast blindly through the now open hole in it. His intent was to drive the Sasquatch back or at least keep it from throwing something else into the cabin at him.

Arey crouched next to Eliza. "She's dead, Lucas!"

Lucas's mind was reeling. Everything was happening so fast.

Something huge and heavy slammed into the cabin's door. Wood cracked, not just the door but the table nailed to it as well. Before Lucas could even move, whatever it was smashed against the door again.

"Marshal!" Deputy Arey snapped at him, moving into a position where she had a clear shot at the door. Her Glock was outstretched in a two-handed grip.

Lucas shook his head as if to clear it and then sprang into action. He worked the pump of his Remington 870, chambering a round, racing to stand next to Arey but with enough space between them so that they wouldn't be in each other's way or line of fire.

The third hit against the door was more than it could take. The Sasquatch burst into the cabin. The great beast roared in a furious rage at them. They answered with hot lead. Lucas's Remington 870 kicked against his shoulder as he squeezed its trigger. Deputy Arey's Glock was firing rapidly as she emptied her magazine into the raging Sasquatch. The heavy slug Lucas shot struck the Sasquatch in its left shoulder, blowing away a chunk of meat there. The 9mm rounds from Arey weren't doing crap against the monster.

The Sasquatch staggered from the wound Lucas inflicted on it but recovered quickly, charging forward. It roared again, somehow even louder than before. Lucas had managed to chamber another round but was forced to throw himself sideways instead of taking a second shot in order to avoid the beast plowing into him. Lucas's dodge was successful as he saw Deputy Arey was on the move too. Ejecting her pistol's spent magazine, she reloaded, staying out of the Sasquatch's reach by retreating in the opposite direction that he had.

"Look out!" Lucas shouted as the Sasquatch made a dive at Arey.

Arey tried to twist away from the monster but it was too fast. A massive hand clutched her shoulder, fingers sinking into her flesh. Blood ran from where they entered. Gritting her teeth, Arey brought up her Glock. Its barrel flashed as she fired directly into the Sasquatch's forehead at point blank range. The bullet squished against the thick bone under the hair there, still not penetrating, but it did knock the beast's head back. Letting go of her, the Sasquatch shook itself like a wet dog.

"Get out of here!" Arey wailed at Lucas. "Someone has to survive this nightmare!"

Lucas wasn't about to leave the tough, little woman to the beast. Raising his Remington 870 and bracing it against his shoulder, Lucas aimed the weapon at the hulking monster. The Sasquatch must have somehow sensed the threat he was to it. With a snarl, it whirled about, lashing out with a clawed hand to knock the barrel of his shotgun aside. A section of the cabin's wall took the blast meant for it. Still snarling, the beast launched itself at Lucas.

With no time to chamber another round, Lucas smashed the butt of his shotgun into the monster's mouth. Two of its teeth broke and blood flew, spattering, from its smashed lower lip. The Sasquatch's snarl became a howl, striking at Lucas, over and over, in a flurry of blows. Lucas couldn't dodge them all. Claws raked across his chest, opening up bloody streaks of torn flesh over his ribs. He fell backwards onto the floor in a desperate attempt to avoid being torn apart.

Arey's Glock was booming as she emptied another magazine into the beast. As the pistol clicked empty, the Sasquatch was very much still standing. The little deputy flung her Glock away in disgust at its ability to hurt the monster. Spotting the axe that Eliza had planned to use against the Sasquatch, Arey ran for the weapon, snatching it up.

Lucas lay on the floor, bleeding and struggling to find the strength to get up, as he watched the Sasquatch leap at Deputy Arey. She met the hulking monster with the axe in her hands. Swinging the weapon in a two-handed grip, with all the force she could muster, Arey hammered its blade into the Sasquatch's chest. The axe's handle snapped in two, leaving the blade stuck where it was. Arey, off balance, was helpless to avoid the Sasquatch. It ignored the axe head and blood running out around. The great beast's claws caught the side of Arey's face, tearing away an eye and most of her cheek. Arey squealed, dropping the broken axe handle. It clattered to the floor at the tough little deputy's feet.

"Run, you idiot. Run!" Arey shouted again at Lucas, blood leaking from her mouth and pouring from her mangled face.

Having fought his way to his feet, this time Lucas listened to her. He stumbled towards the door without looking back. Arey had made her choice. She was going to die in the hope that he could escape and live. Arey shrieked inside the cabin but her cry was suddenly silenced by the sound of tearing flesh. Something struck Lucas in the back as he continued forward and bounced off of him. The impact sent him crashing to the ground. Fresh waves of pain rippled through his torn up chest. Grimacing and biting his lip, Lucas looked over to see Arey's head lying in the grass. Her mouth was open, eyes wide. The beast had pulled the deputy's head from her shoulders and thrown it at him like a rock. Then things took a turn Lucas hadn't seen coming.

"Stay down!" Sheriff Roland's voice ordered him.

Lucas looked toward the trees to see the sheriff and over half a dozen more men emerging from them. Their weapons came up as the Sasquatch roared and bolted out of the cabin at them. A cacophony of gunfire erupted. Shotguns, AR-15s, and rifles let loose. The tide of bullets ripped at the Sasquatch, shredding and tearing its flesh. A couple of shotgun blasts opened up the beast's stomach. Purple, red slicked strands of intestines poured out, dangling limply like dead snakes. AR rounds slammed into the Sasquatch all over its body. While they didn't all get real penetration through the dense muscles of the Sasquatch, they still had to hurt all hell. Other shotgun blasts ripped chunks of meat from the great beast as it thrashed about, unable to continue forward towards the men. One guy in a deputy's uniform with a high powered hunting rifle made the killing shot. The round he fired struck the Sasquatch in the head, punching through its skull, to splatter the great beast's brains out over the grass. The Sasquatch's massive body collapsed with a thud and lay on the ground in front of the cabin.

Several men rushed forward, surrounding the downed Sasquatch, guns aimed at it.

"Whooee! What the hell is this critter?" one redneck shouted.

"It stinks to high heavens," another with a disgusted expression waved at the air in front of his face as if trying to shoo away the beast's smell.

"It's got be one of them there Bigfeet!" another

exclaimed.

"We're gonna be famous, boys!" the first guy who had spoken now whooped.

A man wearing an EMT uniform and Sheriff Roland hurried over to Lucas. The rough hands of the EMT rolled him over. He heard the man suck in a stunned breath at the sight of his chest.

"Stay still!" the EMT ordered, helping Lucas to roll over. "You're torn up pretty bad but you'll live."

"Where's everyone else?" Sheriff Roland asked.

"Dead," Lucas answered. "Everyone else is dead."

Sheriff Roland towered over him and the EMT working on his wounded chest.

"Hedrick?" The sheriff questioned him as if not comprehending what he'd just said or like it hadn't sunk in yet.

"Roland. . ." Lucas winced as the EMT tightened a section of the bandages. "He's dead. They're all dead. . . even Dearil Horror."

"That thing. . .it killed them?" Roland asked.

"Bit straight into Dearil's skull," Lucas told the sheriff. "Tore the others apart. Arey's body is in the cabin along with that of a girl we rescued from Dearil. The others are scattered all over these woods."

"Fragging hell," Sheriff Roland shook his head

and then looked back at the body of the Sasquatch. "And that thing. . .?"

"It's just what it looks like it is, Sheriff," Lucas nodded. "It's a Sasquatch or at least something so close you might as well call it that."

"I'm looking straight at it and still don't believe what I am seeing, Marshal," Sheriff Roland confessed.

"I know exactly how you feel, Sheriff," Lucas assured him.

"You gonna be able to walk out of here?" Sheriff Roland looked at Lucas's bandaged up chest.

The EMT answered before he could. "Yeah, he should be."

Lucas realized he recognized the EMT. He had been at the diner where the nightmare that just ended had begun.

"What about Debra?" the EMT asked, his voice cracking ever so slightly.

"She's dead," Lucas told him, repeating himself again. "I'm sorry."

The EMT nodded sadly and didn't say anything else.

Sheriff Roland took a step closer and offered Lucas a hand up. Lucas accepted it and allowed Roland to help pull him onto his feet.

"We're gonna need to take that thing back with us," Lucas said, nodding at the Sasquatch's corpse.

"We can't chance leaving it out here. No one is ever going to believe any of this crap without it."

"Yep," Sheriff Roland agreed. "I'm with you there. The thing looks to be mostly muscle and heavy as hell. I'll get some men to put together something to haul it out of here on. In the meantime, you get what rest you can. That's an order, Marshal."

Lucas chuckled. A local sheriff had no authority over a federal marshal but Lucas was going to listen to Roland anyway.

"You got it, Sheriff," Lucas smirked.

The sun was fully up by the time the group got moving. It'd taken a while to construct a stretcher strong enough to haul the Sasquatch's corpse on. Lucas wasn't complaining though. The rest he'd gotten had done him good. Despite the wounds on his chest, he felt better and was ready to get the hell out of the woods.

The men formed up into a loose formation with Lucas and the sheriff in its center and the four men, one of them the EMT who had been Debra's partner, hauling the Sasquatch behind them. There were two armed men up ahead of them and another covering the rear.

"Where the hell do you think that thing came from, Marshal?" Sheriff Roland asked. "You called it a Sasquatch but do you think it's an alien or something?"

Lucas shook his head in the negative. "No. I think that thing has been here for its entire life. I'd guess it was born in these woods and has always called them home."

"You sound like Trevor," Sheriff Roland tried to laugh but it didn't come out right. Lucas could see that the sheriff was struggling with losing so many people on his watch and couldn't blame him for that.

"He may have been off his head but the guy sure knew these woods," Lucas said in an attempt to comfort the sheriff.

"Off his head?" Sheriff Roland glared at Lucas. "Trevor was right. He was right about it all and not one of us listened to him."

Lucas could only nod in agreement. "Can't blame ourselves though. Monsters like the one those guys are dragging aren't supposed to exist in the real world."

"At least that thing is dead," Sheriff Roland breathed a sigh of relief. "Guess we showed up just in time."

"Sooner would have been better," Lucas reminded the sheriff.

"Yeah," Sheriff Roland nodded solemnly. "I guess it would have."

"But like you said," Lucas tried again to be uplifting. "That thing is dead. . . and so is Dearil

Horror. We've made the world a better place."

Sheriff Roland grunted.

The group was making good time given the effort it took to move the dead Sasquatch. Lucas realized they weren't heading back the way he and his group had come. The diner was in another direction.

Lucas turned his head towards the sheriff. "Where are we. . .?"

"Going?" Sheriff Roland finished for him. "I didn't think a city guy like yourself would notice but yeah, Marshal, we're not heading back to the diner. There are some back roads up in these woods. Old gravel deals. Most folks don't even remember they exist. There's one just a mile or so ahead. The trucks we got here in are there. If it hadn't been for those roads you likely wouldn't be alive right now. They're the only reason we got to you as soon as we did."

"I see," Lucas smiled. "Glad to hear it too."

"You look like you could do with sitting a spell, Marshal," Sheriff Roland smirked. "I can't figure out how you're even still standing up given the hell you must've been through, not to mention. . ."

"My chest looked a lot worse than it was. Most of the damage is superficial and that EMT pumped me full of pain killers," Lucas underplayed how bad he was actually feeling. "Uh, Sheriff, you mind letting me carry your sidearm? I feel kind of naked without a gun."

"After being out here with that thing stalking you," Sheriff Roland smiled, "I can't imagine what that had to be like. You'll be getting P.T.S.D. therapy for the rest of your life."

Lucas held out his hand, "That sounded like a yes."

"Sure," Sheriff Roland drew the gun holstered on his belt. It wasn't a pistol but rather a .44 magnum revolver. He passed it over to Lucas.

Lucas hefted the weapon, feeling its weight. "Nice. Bet this thing has got some kick to it."

"Oh yeah," Sheriff Roland beamed. "Makes nice big holes in things too."

Lucas managed a smile. "Thanks."

"No problem," Sheriff Roland assured him. "I will be wanting it back though."

The group reached their destination, emerging from the woods onto a dirt road. Waiting for them there were two more men armed with hunting rifles who had stayed behind to make sure Dearil couldn't just show up and steal one of the trucks. There were four in all, all of them big, powerful vehicles that could handle the rough terrain. The two men were startled by the monster the group dragged out onto the road with them.

Night was falling quickly. The rays of the sun

were sinking, becoming blocked out by the mountains and the trees. There was still enough light to see but there wouldn't be for long. Sheriff Roland's men set about deciding which truck would be best to load the Sasquatch corpse onto. Lucas leaned against the side of a black Ford F-150 and let himself relax a bit. He really fragging wanted a cigarette. A bunch of the deputies and drafted redneck guys were smoking or chewing which didn't make fighting the longing in him any easier. Lucas bit his lip and tried to think about something else. Against all odds, he'd survived a head on battle with a primal monster that wasn't supposed to really exist. He was going home to Kristen. Lucas missed her so much. Two years might have passed since they got married but in many ways the two of them were still newlyweds. Their passion and love burned bright between them.

The EMT came over to him. "You okay, Marshal?"

Lucas, lost in his thoughts of his wife, didn't respond.

"Marshal?" the EMT said again.

"What?" Lucas blinked and looked at the EMT.

"I asked if you were okay?" there was deep concern in the EMT's voice.

"Yeah. Yeah, I am fine," Lucas told him. "Forgive me but I can't remember your name."

"Easton," the EMT laughed. "Hell man, if I were you I wouldn't remember my own name after all the crap you've been through."

"Thanks, Easton," Lucas moved a bit so that Easton could lean against the side of the truck next to him. "Sorry again about Debra."

"I know you lost your partner too," Easton frowned. "It fragging sucks. Debra was a good woman."

Lucas nodded. "It really does. Stephen was like a brother to me."

The two of them watched a bunch of Roland's other men in the group trying to get the Sasquatch corpse up into the bed of the largest truck. It wasn't going well. The thing was so heavy that Lucas wondered if they were going to be able to do it at all without some kind of lift to move the beast.

Sheriff Roland swaggered over to where Lucas and Easton were.

"You boys taking it easy?" the big man grinned.

"Happy to be getting the hell out of here," Lucas smiled.

One of the men trying to hoist the dead Sasquatch cried out, hurting his back.

"Sheesh," Sheriff Roland shook his head. "I guess I should head over there. Clearly, those boys need some supervising."

"Sheriff," Lucas stopped him. "I want to ask

you something."

"Sure, Marshal," Sheriff Roland said. "What ya want to know?"

A roar sounded from somewhere to the south of where the truck sat on the gravel road. It was followed almost instantly by another somewhere to the west.

"What the hell?" Sheriff Roland stammered.

Lucas stood straight upright. The revolver the sheriff had given him was clutched so tightly his knuckles went white.

"There are more of them," Lucas barked at Sheriff Roland. "Get your men ready. They'll be coming."

"You can't be serious," Sheriff Roland shook his head. "How could there be more?"

"Sheriff!" Lucas snapped. "Get your head out of your butt, man! Don't you get it? We're about to be attacked."

The other men had stopped trying to load the Sasquatch body into the largest truck and were all standing around, looking at the trees. All of them had retrieved their weapons from where they had been put down. Every single person on the road was tensed up and wondering just what in the hell was happening.

Easton wasn't armed. The EMT's face was pale, his eyes wide with fear. "Marshal. . ."

"Get in the truck," Lucas ordered. "And lock the doors."

Lucas knew the EMT wouldn't really be safe in the truck. The beasts that were coming were more than capable of ripping the doors right off the vehicle. If they wanted Easton, there would be no escaping them.

Easton did as he was told, scampering into the Ford F-150 and slamming the door behind him. Lucas hoped Easton would be okay but knew the EMT likely wouldn't be.

The beasts came without further warning. There were more than just the two whose roars had been heard. Two of the things moved in from the west, three more from the south, blocking the road as they charged up it.

Sheriff Roland took charge of things at last. "Hank, Derrick, Marcus, nail those bastards coming up the road. The rest of you target the others! We can't let those things close in on us!"

The three men attempting to fend off the creatures bounding up the road from the south let loose, their guns blazing. Hank's AR-15 chattered while Marcus's shotgun boomed. Derrick had his rifle braced against his shoulder, taking time with his aim. When he did, the high powered round Derrick fired hammered into the forehead of one of the Sasquatch, dropping it dead. There was a gaping exit hole in the rear of the beast's skull as its body thudded onto the gravel road. The Sasquatch were fast as Hell though, closing the distance between them and the men quickly. One of the beasts plowed into Marcus, knocking him from his feet. Before Marcus could roll out of the monster's path or try to get up, a large foot came crashing down. His ribs folded inward, breaking inside of his chest. Bloody spittle flew from Marcus's lips in a grunt of pain. The monster didn't stop there though, bringing its foot down on the man several more times, each breaking more of his bones and making damn sure Marcus was dead. The other monster came straight at Derrick. He worked the bolt of his rifle, chambering a fresh round, and was able to get off a second shot. Unable to properly aim with the Sasquatch almost on top of him, the bullet he fired slammed into the monster's left arm. Blood splattered as it punched through thick hair, flesh, and dense muscle. The Sasquatch roared, taking a swing at Derrick with the clenched fist of its right hand. Derrick tried to dodge the blow but the monster was too fast. It caught the side of his head, stunning Derrick. His ears were ringing and vision blurred as Derrick vainly tried to stumble away from the great beast. The Sasquatch struck again, smashing its fist into Derrick's back. The force of the blow crumbled his spine, spinning it in two inside of Derrick. He continued to stumble a few more steps, carried on by his momentum, and then fell face first into the gravel of the road. Hank was left alone facing two of the monsters. He whirled to engage the closer of the two. His AR-15 peppered its body with bloody spots where bullets tried to penetrate the Sasquatch's muscles. The beast, one arm wounded by Derrick, drew to a halt, raising its good arm in an attempt to block Hank's fire from hitting its face. The other Sasquatch though had nothing to stop it. Flanking Hank, it went into a frenzy, clawed hands lashing out in a flurry of strikes that shredded the flesh of Hank's shoulders, arms, and the left side of his face. Hank went down screaming.

Sheriff Roland, Marshal Lucas, and the remaining three men held their ground against the two Sasquatch that had emerged from the woods to the west of the road while Easton cowered inside the cab of the F-150 he'd been ordered to get into. Two of the men were armed with AR-15s. The chatter of their weapons was deafening as they poured all the bullets they could into the approaching pair of Sasquatch. The third man had a shotgun, as did Sheriff Roland. It was their fire that gave the beasts pause. The lead Sasquatch took a shotgun slug to its lower right side and was staggered by it. The other Sasquatch lost a chunk of its right thigh to a blast from Sheriff Roland. Neither of the Sasquatch were fully stopped by the barrage of hot lead. They kept coming, lips parted in feral snarls and yellow eyes burning with rage.

Lucas hadn't fired a shot. He knew there were only six rounds in the Magnum that Sheriff Roland had given him. Making them count seemed like a good idea. Lucas had fought a Sasquatch before and knew the others likely weren't going to stop the monsters. He broke from the sheriff and the others, racing around the truck.

"Marshal!" Sheriff Roland shouted at him, anger in his voice at being deserted.

The pair of Sasquatch and the remaining two coming up the road all closed in on the sheriff and his last three men. One of Roland's men successfully managed to kill another of the monsters but lost his life in the process. A Sasquatch snatched the man into a bear hug, lifting him from the ground. As it did, the man shoved the barrel of his shotgun into the hulking beast's mouth and squeezed the trigger. The top of the Sasquatch's head exploded in a shower of gore. As the beast died, its arms went so tight against the man's body, pressing him to its chest, that his insides were crushed.

Another of Sheriff Roland's men didn't have a chance in hell as a Sasquatch rushed him. The beast brought its massive clenched fists together on the man's head, doing the same as had happened to the head of the Sasquatch ahead of it. His headless corpse collapsed onto the gravel road.

The last of Roland's men trying to hold the Sasquatch back kept firing his AR-15. Round after round hammered at the chest and wide shoulders of the beast coming right at him. The bullets stung the monster but did little more. It took a swing at the man. Somehow, he was able to move fast enough to duck the blow and come back up with his AR blazing, point blank into the Sasquatch's groin. The beast howled in pain, reeling backwards away from the man. Seeing his chance, the man tried to make a run for it. Giving the staggering beast a wide berth, the man sprinted past the Sasquatch, heading away from the trucks, down the road. To Lucas, it looked as if the man might actually make it and escape the battle that was ending but then a sixth Sasquatch, possibly a female one as it was smaller and slimmer than the others, bounded out of the trees into his path. Before the man could bring his AR-15 into play, the six foot tall Sasquatch struck. Its hairy hand entered him, punching through his rib cage to emerge through his back. The female beast yanked its hand free from the man's body and threw back her head, screeching at the sky.

There was no way Sheriff Roland was running though. He stood tough and tall, holding his ground against impossible odds, determined to send more of the monsters to hell. Working the pump of his shotgun to chamber another round, Sheriff Roland took aim at the closest of the snarling Sasquatch. The shotgun thundered as he put a round into its throat. Its snarling becoming a sickening gargling noise, the Sasquatch stopped, hands clutching the mangled flesh from the heavy round that poured rivers of red down into the hair of its chest. Sheriff Roland worked the weapon's pump again, spinning about to face another of the beasts coming at him from his right side. With another carefully aimed shot, he blew the hell out of the monster's left knee. The Sasquatch went down, rolling on the gravel. Sheriff Roland moved quickly to dodge it and then put a second round into the Sasquatch's face, sending its blood splattering all over his legs and lower body.

The sheriff was one fragging tough mother, Lucas thought, watching him. The federal marshal scampered into the bed of the truck that Easton was in. He thumped on the window behind the EMT, getting his attention. Easton turned in the driver's seat to gawk at him.

"Crank up and get us the hell out of here!" Lucas yelled, thumping on the window again to drive his point home.

"I don't have the keys!" Easton wailed.

"Hot wire the damn thing then!" Lucas snapped. A Sasquatch had broken away from the fight going on with Sheriff Roland and was bounding towards the truck. Raising his Magnum in a double-handed grip, Lucas squeezed off a round that pulped the beast's right eye in its socket, using that as an entrance to its brain. The Sasquatch's head jerked back atop its neck as the bullet struck and the creature died instantly.

The two beasts still engaged by Sheriff Roland circled him. The sheriff had run out of ammo. He was now holding his shotgun like a ball bat, waiting for one of the creatures to make the first move. Lucas felt a stab of guilt as he was clutching the sheriff's sidearm in his own hands. He wanted to help the sheriff but didn't dare risk drawing the attention of the beasts to the truck before Easton could get it moving. Lucas watched helplessly as the sheriff made his last stand.

Sheriff Roland swung his shotgun at the first Sasquatch to lunge at him. The shotgun smashed into the creature's mouth, knocking loose a jagged tooth and sending blood squirting from its lower lip where the gun's butt met it. The beast wasn't knocked back though. Massive, hair-covered hands grabbed the sheriff; one ripped away his left arm from his shoulder as the other crushed the upper part of his right.

The engine finally roared to life as the truck lurched under Lucas's feet. Easton had managed to get it started and floored the gas. Unable to remain standing, Lucas sunk, grabbing hold of the side of its bed. Gravel flew as the wheels spun out and the truck surged forward. It wasn't facing the direction that led down out of the woods. Easton fought with the steering wheel, righting its path, with one hell of a big swerve. All of the Sasquatch were rushing towards the vehicle now but only the female was close enough to reach it. One of her hands grabbed hold of the tailgate, fingers crunching its metal beneath the pressure of her grip. With a mighty heave and a jump, she sprang up into the truck bed with Lucas. The truck's struts and shocks were strained to their limits from her weight landing on them. The impact nearly made Easton lose control of the vehicle as it sped away from the other Sasquatch. Easton kept control though and the truck pointed down the mountain. Lucas's Magnum boomed three times like claps of thunder. The rounds he fired hit the female beast in the center of her chest between her sagging, hair-covered breasts, throwing her off balance. Stumbling back, she fell over the edge of the truck bed, landing roughly on the gravel road and bouncing along it. Lucas leaped to his feet, relieved that the beast was gone. He never saw the low hanging tree limb that took his life. Bone crunched as his skull was caved in by the wood, leaving a bloody smear and bits of hair on its bark.

****

Several hours later, Easton sat at a foldout table inside a tent near the diner where Dearil Horror had escaped. An older federal marshal, with streaks of gray in his hair, named Ross paced in front of him.

"You can't seriously expect me to believe what you're claiming," Ross growled.

"I don't give a damn what you believe or not, Marshal," Easton said. "What I told you is the truth."

"That a bunch of monsters killed my men, the locals who were assisting them, and even Dearil Horror too?" Ross shook his head in disgust. "Either you must think I am a complete fool or you're on something, son."

"Look, sir, my answers aren't changing," Easton leaned forward, "And I am telling you, somebody needs to go out there and wipe those monsters out before they get braver. If they ever come out of those woods in force. . ."

"Then what?" Ross eyed the EMT closely.

"You'll have a war on your hands, sir," Easton told him. "And the streets of the small towns in this area will be drenched in blood."

"Get him out of here!" Ross barked at one of his underlings that was waiting just outside the tent's entrance.

Rough hands tugged Easton up and out of his chair and forced him out.

The old man had stopped pacing. As he lit up a fat cigar, puffing on it, Ross muttered to himself, "A Bigfoot War. Where the hell do people come up with this crap?"

The EMT hadn't been any help at all beyond giving them an idea of where to look for Marshal Lucas and the sheriff. Still, that was a start. Ross sucked smoke into his lungs and exhaled it slowly before walking outside to see whether the group his people had been putting together was ready to head into the woods yet. He looked up as a copter flew overhead. It had taken a while to get one to the area, given how rural and out of the way it was, but at least the bird was here now. Ross figured having it would help a lot in locating both Dearil and the others. Regardless, the night was almost over and the sun would be coming up soon. It was time to get moving no matter what was waiting for them in the woods.

THE END

Author Bio

Eric S Brown is the author of numerous book series including the Bigfoot War series, the Psi-Mechs Inc. series, the Kaiju Apocalypse series (with Jason Cordova), the Crypto-Squad series (with Jason Brannon), the Homeworld series (With Tony Faville and Jason Cordova), the Jack Bunny Bam series, and the A Pack of Wolves series. Some of his stand alone books include War of the Worlds plus Blood Guts and Zombies, Casper Alamo (with Jason Brannon), Sasquatch Island, Day of the Sasquatch, Bigfoot, Crashed, World War of the Dead, Last Stand in a Dead Land, Sasquatch Lake, Kaiju Armageddon, Megalodon, Megalodon Apocalypse, Kraken, Alien Battalion, The Last Fleet, and From the Snow They Came to name only a few. His short fiction has been published hundreds of times in the small press in beyond including markets like the Onward Drake and Black Tide Rising anthologies from Baen Books, the Grantville Gazette, the SNAFU Military horror anthology series, and Walmart World magazine. He has done the novelizations for such films as Boggy Creek: The Legend is True (Studio 3 Entertainment) and The Bloody Rage of Bigfoot (Great Lake films). The first book of his Bigfoot War series was adapted into a feature film by Origin Releasing in 2014. Werewolf Massacre at Hell's Gate was the second of his books to be adapted into film in 2015. Major Japanese publisher, Takeshobo, bought the reprint rights to his Kaiju Apocalypse series (with Jason Cordova) and the mass market, Japanese language version was released in late 2017. Ring of Fire Press has released a collected edition of his Monster Society stories (set in the New York Times Best-selling world of Eric Flint's 1632). In addition to his fiction, Eric also writes an award-winning comic book news column entitled "Comics in a Flash" as well a pop culture column for Altered Reality Magazine. Eric lives in North Carolina with his wife and two children where he continues to write tales of the hungry dead, blazing guns, and the things that lurk in the woods.

Check out other great
Cryptid Novels!

J.H. Moncrieff
RETURN TO DYATLOV PASS

In 1959, nine Russian students set off on a skiing expedition in the Ural Mountains. Their mutilated bodies were discovered weeks later. Their bizarre and unexplained deaths are one of the most enduring true mysteries of our time. Nearly sixty years later, podcast host Nat McPherson ventures into the same mountains with her team, determined to finally solve the mystery of the Dyatlov Pass incident. Her plans are thwarted on the first night, when two trackers from her group are brutally slaughtered. The team's guide, a superstitious man from a neighboring village, blames the killings on yetis, but no one believes him. As members of Nat's team die one by one, she must figure out if there's a murderer in their midst—or something even worse—before history repeats itself and her group becomes another casualty of the infamous Dead Mountain.

Gerry Griffiths
CRYPTID ZOO

As a child, rare and unusual animals, especially cryptid creatures, always fascinated Carter Wilde. Now that he's an eccentric billionaire and runs the largest conglomerate of high-tech companies all over the world, he can finally achieve his wildest dream of building the most incredible theme park ever conceived on the planet... CRYPTID ZOO. Even though there have been apparent problems with the project, Wilde still decides to send some of his marketing employees and their families on a forced vacation to assess the theme park in preparation for Opening Day. Nick Wells and his family are some of those chosen and are about to embark on what will become the most terror-filled weekend of their lives—praying they survive. STEP RIGHT UP AND GET YOUR FREE PASS... TO CRYPTID ZOO

Check out other great

Cryptid Novels!

Hunter Shea

LOCH NESS REVENGE

Deep in the murky waters of Loch Ness, the creature known as Nessie has returned. Twins Natalie and Austin McQueen watched in horror as their parents were devoured by the world's most infamous lake monster. Two decades later, it's their turn to hunt the legend. But what lurks in the Loch is not what they expected. Nessie is devouring everything in and around the Loch, and it's not alone. Hell has come to the Scottish Highlands. In a fierce battle between man and monster, the world may never be the same. Praise for THEY RISE : "Outrageous, balls to the wall...made me yearn for 3D glasses and a tub of popcorn, extra butter!" – The Eyes of Madness "A fast-paced, gore-heavy splatter fest of sharksploitation." The Werd "A rocket paced horror story. I enjoyed the hell out of this book." Shotgun Logic Reviews

C.G. Mosley

BAKER COUNTY BIGFOOT CHRONICLE

Marie Bledsoe only wants her missing brother Kurt back. She'll stop at nothing to make it happen and, with the help of Kurt's friend Tony, along with Sheriff Ray Cochran, Marie embarks on a terrifying journey deep into the belly of the mysterious Walker Laboratory to find him. However, what she and her companions find lurking in the laboratory basement is beyond comprehension. There are cryptids from the forest being held captive there and something...else. Enjoy this suspenseful tale from the mind of C.G. Mosley, author of Wood Ape. Welcome back to Baker County, a place where monsters do lurk in the night!

SEVERED**PRESS**

🐦 @severedpress
f /severedpress

Check out other great

Cryptid Novels!

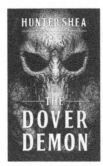

Hunter Shea

THE DOVER DEMON

The Dover Demon is real...and it has returned. In 1977, Sam Brogna and his friends came upon a terrifying, alien creature on a deserted country road. What they witnessed was so bizarre, so chilling, they swore their silence. But their lives were changed forever. Decades later, the town of Dover has been hit by a massive blizzard. Sam's son, Nicky, is drawn to search for the infamous cryptid, only to disappear into the bowels of a secret underground lair. The Dover Demon is far deadlier than anyone could have believed. And there are many of them. Can Sam and his reunited friends rescue Nicky and battle a race of creatures so powerful, so sinister, that history itself has been shaped by their secretive presence? "THE DOVER DEMON is Shea's most delightful and insidiously terrifying monster yet." – Shotgun Logic Reviews "An excellent horror novel and a strong standout in the UFO and cryptid subgenres. –Hellnotes "Non-stop action awaits those brave enough to dive into the small town of Dover, and if you're lucky, you won't see the Demon himself!" – The Scary Reviews PRAISE FOR SWAMP MONSTER MASSACRE "B-horror movie fans rejoice, Hunter Shea is here to bring you the ultimate tale of terror!" – Horror Novel Reviews "A nonstop thrill ride! I couldn't put this book down." – Cedar Hollow Horror Reviews

Armand Rosamilia

THE BEAST

The end of summer, 1986. With only a few days left until the new school year, twins Jeremy and Jack Schaffer are on very different paths. Jeremy is the geek, playing Dungeons & Dragons with friends Kathleen and Randy, while Jack is the jock, getting into trouble with his buddies. And then everything changes when neighbor Mister Higgins is killed by a wild animal in his yard. Was it a bear? There's something big lurking in the woods behind their New Jersey home. Will the police be able to solve the murder before more Middletown residents are ripped apart?

Check out other great

Cryptid Novels!

P.K. Hawkins

THE CRYPTID FILES

Fresh out of the academy with top marks, Agent Bradley Tennyson is expecting to have the pick of cases and investigations throughout the country. So he's shocked when instead he is assigned as the new partner to "The Crag," an agent well past his prime. He thinks the assignment is a punishment. It's anything but.Agent George Crag has been doing this job for far longer than most, and he knows what skeletons his bosses have in the closet and where the bodies are buried. He has pretty much free reign to pick his cases, and he knows exactly which one he wants to use to break in his new young partner: the disappearance and murder of a couple of college kids in a remote mountain town.Tennyson doesn't realize it, but Crag is about to introduce him to a world he never believed existed: The Cryptid Files, a world of strange monsters roaming in the night. Because these murders have been going on for a long time, and evidence is mounting that the murderer may just in fact be the legendary Bigfoot.

Gerry Griffiths

DOWN FROM BEAST MOUNTAIN

A beast with a grudge has come down from the mountain to terrorize the townsfolk of Porterville. The once sleepy town is suddenly wide awake. Sheriff Abel McGuire and game warden Grant Tanner frantically investigate one brutal slaying after another as they follow the blood trail they hope will eventually lead to the monstrous killer. But they better hurry and stop the carnage before the census taker has to come out and change the population sign on the edge of town to ZERO.

Check out other great

Cryptid Novels!

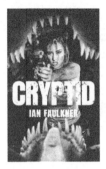

Ian Faulkner

CRYPTID

Be careful what you look for. You might just find it.1996. A group of 14 students walked into the trackless virgin forests of Graham Island, British Columbia for a three-day hike. They were never seen again. 2019. An American TV crew retrace those students' steps to attempt to solve a 23-year-old mystery.A disparate collection of characters arrives on the island. But all is not as it seems. Two of them carry dark secrets. Terrible knowledge that will mean death for some – but a fighting chance of survival for others. In the hidden depths of the forests – man is on the menu. Some mysteries should remain unsolved...

Eric S. Brown

LOCH NESS HORROR

The Order of the Eternal Light, a secret organization have foretold the end of the human race. In order to save all humanity, agents of the Order must locate the Loch Ness Monster and obtain a sample of its blood for within in it is the key to stopping the apocalypse but finding the monster will be no easy task.

Made in the USA
Las Vegas, NV
27 December 2023

83558365R00079